Magical Celtic Tales

First published 2016 by
The O'Brien Press Ltd,
12 Terenure Road East, Rathgar,
Dublin 6, D06 HD27, Ireland.
Tel: +353 1 4923333; Fax: +353 1 4922777
E-mail: books@obrien.ie
Website: www.obrien.ie

ISBN: 978-1-84717-546-5

1 3 5 7 8 6 4 2
16 18 20 19 17

Printed and bound in Poland by Białostockie Zakłady Graficzne S.A.
The paper in this book is produced using pulp from managed forests.

Published in

DUBLIN

UNESCO
City of Literature

Magical
Celtic Tales

Una Leavy

Illustrated by Fergal O'Connor

THE O'BRIEN PRESS
DUBLIN

FOR JUDE

CONTENTS

INTRODUCTION

When I was growing up I liked nothing better than reading. My favourite stories were the ancient Irish legends. Some I first read in old books belonging to my grandfather, stories in which strange things happened to ordinary people. There were tales of mystery and magic, trickery and enchantment that kept me spellbound. I soon noticed, however, that other countries had very similar tales. It was then that I discovered the Celts.

Long ago, tribes known as Celts lived and fought all over continental Europe. Eventually, somewhere around 500 BC, they began to arrive in Britain and Ireland. They were conquered in Britain by the Romans and other invaders. They continued to live there all the same, mainly in Scotland, Wales, Cornwall and The Isle of Man. Some settled in Brittany, in northwest France. As the Romans did not bother much with Ireland, the Celts flourished there, and their language and many of their customs continue to this day.

We don't really know for sure where the Celts came from. Some say from here, some from there. Others think they weren't a race at all, just tribes who shared the same traditions and culture. Whatever their true history, you can trace them in the landscape, place names and language wherever they settled, and you can see their jewellery in several National Museums. In all the countries where the Celts lived, they told wonderful stories, some of which are collected in this book. I hope you enjoy them as much as people did when they first heard them many centuries ago.

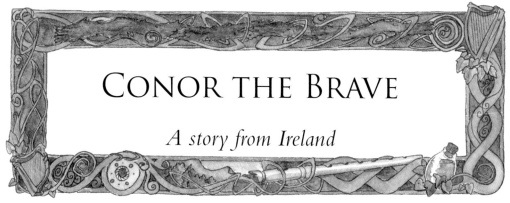

CONOR THE BRAVE

A story from Ireland

Long ago in Ireland lived a poor widow who had one son named Conor. All he had to wear were patched trousers and a tattered, sheepskin jacket. Since his clothes were ragged, his mother kept him from school, so he never learned fractions, decimals or percentages.

Early one morning, Conor's mother called him.

'Conor,' she said, 'the fire is out and I cannot boil the kettle.'

'I'll go to the forest for firewood,' said Conor at once.

'Oh, no!' cried his mother. 'Strange things happen there and something might hurt you.'

'Don't worry, mother,' Conor said. 'I'm not afraid of anything.'

He set off with his axe. Hedges drooped with fuchsia, sunlight dappled the grass, but the forest was dim with shadow. Whistling as he worked, he soon collected a pile of firewood. As he turned for home, a fierce giant hopped out before him. In his hand was a huge, twisted stick.

'Here comes breakfast!' the giant grinned. 'You'll just fit on my frying-pan.' In a cat's wink, Conor tripped the giant, and tied him up in tangles.

'Boo hoo hoo!' sobbed the giant, 'please don't kill me, please don't kill me!'

'What will you give me if I spare your life?' Conor asked.

'Take my stick,' cried the giant. 'You'll never be beaten as long as you have it.'

So Conor released the giant. Then taking the stick he skipped home through the forest.

All was well for a time. But one day, Conor's mother called him again.

'Conor,' she said, 'the fire is out and I cannot fry the boxty.'

'I'll go to the forest for firewood,' said Conor at once.

'Oh, no!' cried his mother. 'Wicked things happen there and something might harm you.'

'Don't worry, mother,' Conor said. 'I'm not afraid of anything.'

He set off with his axe. Bees buzzed in the bushes, cats dozed in the heat, but in the forest it was icy cold. Humming as he worked, he soon collected a pile of firewood. As he turned for home, a fierce giant with two heads jumped out before him. From his pocket peeped a silver fife.

'Here comes lunch!' the giant sneered. 'You'll just fit in my saucepan.'

In a dog's wag, Conor tripped the giant and tied him up knots.

'Hoo boo hoo!' sobbed the giant, 'please don't kill me, please don't kill me!'

'What will you give me if I spare your life?' Conor asked.

'Take my fife,' cried the giant. 'Whoever hears its music will never stop dancing.'

So Conor released the giant. Then taking the fife, he hopped home through the forest.

All was well for a time. Then one night, Conor's mother called him.

'Conor,' she said, 'the fire is out and I cannot bake the soda bread.'

'I'll go to the forest for firewood,' said Conor at once.

'Oh, no!' cried his mother. 'Evil things happen there and something might kill you.'

'Don't worry, mother,' Conor said. 'I'm not afraid of anything.'

He set off with his axe. A half moon glittered, the night was still, but the forest hissed with whispers. Singing as he worked, he soon collected a pile of wood. As he turned for home, a fierce giant with three heads leaped out of the shadows. On his belt hung a dark green bottle.

'Here comes supper!' the giant roared. 'You'll just fit on my barbecue!'

In a hen's peck, Conor tripped the giant and tied him up in twists.

'Boo boo hoo!' sobbed the giant, 'please don't kill me, please don't kill me!'

'What will you give me if I spare your life?' Conor asked.

'Take the green bottle,' cried the giant. 'The ointment in it will keep you safe from fire.'

So Conor released the giant. Then taking the bottle he trotted home through the forest.

Well, all this giant business gave Conor courage. Next evening he went down to the village. In his pockets were the stick, the fife and the dark green bottle. People stared at his clothes, children pointed and laughed. But Conor didn't care. He was too busy listening to a stranger talking in the square.

'The King of Leinster is in trouble,' announced the stranger. 'His beautiful daughter has not laughed for seven years. Kings and princes have tried in vain. She says she will marry any man who can make her laugh.'

'I'm the man,' thought Conor, as he set off for Leinster.

When he got to the king's fort, there was nobody at the gate. Everyone was in the enclosure, strolling around and watching games. There were hurlers hurling, and poets droning, and pipers playing tunes. Among them sat the princess with her father. Conor watched her. She didn't smile once, but he couldn't stop staring.

Eventually, a sentry marched towards him.

'Clear off, fool!' he yelled. 'You're not fit to be seen by a princess!'

Seven warriors surrounded him, drawing their spears. Conor swung the giant's stick lightly round his shoulders. The warriors tumbled to the ground. They lay on their backs in a circle, legs waving like wasps. Nobody moved or spoke. Then in the silence came a tiny chuckle. All heads turned to look at the princess. With hands at her mouth, she tried to hide a smile.

'Now, o king,' said Conor bravely, 'I've made your daughter laugh. She's quarter mine already.'

'Says who?' answered the princess, tossing back her hair. But she whispered something in the king's ear.

Conor was invited to supper. You can't sit with a princess without making some effort. So they let him wash himself and gave him proper clothes. He hoped they might even let him sit beside the girl. Not so. Her father sat on one side and a thin man with orange hair sat down on the other. 'Foxface' was the name Conor called him to himself. Foxface smiled at the princess, pouring drinks and telling jokes. The princess didn't laugh once.

The king turned to Conor.

'We have a problem in our kingdom,' he sighed. 'A vicious wolf lives in the woods behind the fort. He prowls around at dawn, killing animals and people. We are all afraid of him.'

'You seem like a brave fellow,' said Foxface to Conor. 'Why not kill the wolf and prove it?'

'No problem,' said Conor, 'just tell me where to find him.'

Foxface smiled an ugly smile; he turned to the king.

'Why don't we leave the gates open tonight?' he suggested. 'The wolf is sure

to come. We'll see how brave this man is then.'

'Oh, keep away from the wolf!' the princess squealed. Then she blushed. 'Well, only if you must.'

Next day, just as the sun rose, Conor sauntered to the yard. The princess arrived with Foxface and her father. Shortly after, the wolf came padding in. He was long and lean, with cunning eyes and pointed teeth. When he saw the cattle in their stalls, he licked his jaws. Foxface stood flat against the wall.

As soon as Conor moved towards him, the wolf crouched. Snarling and bristling, he suddenly pounced. But whipping out the silver fife, Conor began to play. Music pealed and echoed across the yard. All at once, the wolf began to dance! Legs up, paws down, legs up again, round and round he went! Sheep and cattle galloped from their stalls. Hens and chickens fluttered from their roosts. Soon the whole yard was dancing. Up and down, in and out, stomping, leaping, whirling! Foxface danced until he lost his stockings, the princess tittered and giggled.

Conor didn't stop playing till the wolf fell down exhausted.

'Get out of here,' he ordered, 'and if you ever come back ...'

The wolf staggered off with his tail between his legs.

'Well, my fine princess,' said Conor then, 'now you're half mine.'

'We'll see about that!' the princess said, but her eyes were bright.

'Oh, you're smart alright,' said Foxface when he got his breath back, 'but are you smart enough to defeat fighting men? Word has just come - the king's enemies are about to attack. There's only one thing in the world that can defeat them.'

'And what's that?' Conor asked.

'There's a magic blade that can chop off a hundred heads. If we had this blade, our enemies would run.'

'Lead me to it,' Conor said.

'It's not so easy,' Foxface sneered. 'The blade belongs to the Lord of the

Underworld. You must ask him for it. Of course, you might get killed,' he grinned.

'I'll go at once,' said Conor. 'I'm not afraid of anything.'

'Oh, Conor! Please don't go!' said the princess with a sob.

Conor looked into her lovely grey eyes.

'When I return, you're all mine,' he said, not being very good at fractions.

'I'll think about it,' said the princess, but she blushed bright red.

When people heard of Conor's plan, they shook their heads.

'Poor fellow!' they said, 'he won't come back alive. He'll burn forever in a terrible fire.'

Next morning, Conor set off. He travelled miles, stopping at last at a pair of iron gates. Skulls and bones hung from the gateposts. A stench of burning poured through the bars. Conor took out the green bottle. Rubbing his hands with the giant's ointment, he knocked on the gates. A hundred imps' heads appeared.

'What do you want?' they screeched.

'I want to speak to the Lord of the Underworld,' Conor said.

Immediately the gates opened into a hot, murky room. Smoke billowed, sparks spat, flames curled along the walls. Overhead, hanging on a nail, he could see the magic blade.

The Lord of the Underworld came smiling from the gloom.

'I've come to borrow the magic blade,' Conor said. 'The King of Leinster needs it to defeat his enemies.'

'Well now, young man,' said the Lord, as he stroked his chin, 'these enemies are some of my best friends. But since you've come so far, I will let you have it. Hand down the blade,' he winked to the boldest imp. The imp grinned as he took the red-hot blade. He could not wait to see how Conor's hands would burn.

'Thank you,' said Conor, taking it easily. 'Now kindly open the gates.'

The Lord of the Underworld snarled in rage.

'Easier to get in than to get out!' he screeched.

The imps charged at Conor in a screaming mob. But he swung the blade around his shoulders and knocked off their horns.

'Let him out!' screamed the Lord, 'and a curse on anyone who lets him in again!'

People saw Conor returning with the blade, and the news got around. The king's enemies soon heard the tale.

'Conor has the magic blade!' they shrieked. 'He'll chop off our heads! Hurry, hurry, hurry! Let's get out of here!'

So they jumped in their longboats and quickly sailed away.

The king was delighted when Conor returned, but Foxface was furious.

'The princess should be mine,' he thought. 'I'll have that fool's life. She will never be his wife.'

He looked round for a weapon. Seeing the magic blade he snatched it up. Such screeching and screaming! The metal burned his fingers and the blade dropped on his toes. Such flinging of ankles and flittering of feet, such howling and screeching you never heard! The sight of Foxface leaping made the princess burst out laughing. Conor turned and took her hand.

'All mine now, I think,' he said.

'Oh, alright, if you insist,' the princess whispered. So he kissed her.

Well, Conor got tidied up a bit and prepared for the wedding. His mother came to help and they gave him fine clothes. A wise man at the palace taught him fractions and decimals. The princess and Conor were married shortly after. They lived happily in Leinster and are living there still. But he never quite managed to master fractions.

THE SEAL CATCHER'S STORY

A story from Scotland

Long ago and far away, in the north of Scotland, there was a young man named Hamish. He lived with his family in a cottage near the shore. There was Grandfather and Grandmother, Father and Mother, three sisters, two brothers, a cousin and a baby. The men fished a bit and farmed a bit, the women knitted. But they were still very poor.

'I'll have to earn more money,' thought Hamish one day. 'But what can I do? It takes years to become a stone-mason or a blacksmith or a weaver.'

He wandered down to the beach. Seagulls screeched and swooped, waves slapped against the rocks. Sunning themselves on the smoothest stones lay three sleek seals. As Hamish approached, they rolled off into the water.

'Aren't they handsome!' he said to himself. 'Such fine, shiny coats they have, so glossy and dark.'

He paused. Suddenly a thought struck him. He punched the air with his fist.

'That's it!' he shouted. 'I'll be a seal catcher! Rich people buy seal skins for waistcoats and jackets. There are plenty of seals; they'll be easy to catch. I'll sell them to a merchant and soon *I'll* be rich! '

On his way home he thought about the old legend his grandmother often told. It was said that killing seals would bring nothing but bad luck – not that he believed such rubbish. How could killing seals harm anyone? Only people living by the sea believed such nonsense. Still, Hamish decided not to mention it at home. They would only try to stop him.

Next morning he borrowed his father's sharpest knife. Without a word to anyone, he slipped down to the beach. Within hours he was back with a bundle of sealskins. Not one single person was pleased to see him.

'What have you done?' shouted Grandfather.

'You've brought bad luck on us!' sobbed Grandmother.

'You should never kill a seal!' roared Father.

'Throw those skins away!' begged Mother.

'Waaaaaaaaaaah!' wailed the baby who was upset with the racket.

'Now look what you've done!' yelled the sisters and brothers and cousin.

Poor Hamish. That was not at all what he'd expected. But he was a brave lad and stubborn with it. The following day he went to the market. A merchant bought the sealskins for two gold pieces. So Hamish bought his own sharp knife, then set off home with his pockets full of sweeties and presents.

Now Hamish had a whole new life. He no longer went fishing or farming with the others. Every day he hunted seals on the shore, creeping up behind them as they basked in the sun. Each Wednesday he sold the skins at the market. He bought boots for his brothers and cloaks for the girls. He bought plaids for his father and linens for his mother. Grandfather and Grandmother had their own special treats. And as for the baby – she chewed happily on a new rag doll.

Life became easier for Hamish's family. But the older people still worried and fretted.

'Some seals are selkies,' said Grandfather.

'At times they are human,' explained Grandmother.

'It's bad luck to kill them,' warned Father.

'Please stop this at once!' pleaded Mother.

'We don't care,' said the sisters and brothers and cousin, 'keep buying us nice things. Who cares for old tales?'

'Gooo gaaa,' said the baby, who didn't care either.

And neither did Hamish. Everyone in the cottage was stronger and healthier. They had warm clothes for winter and plenty to eat. Soon he would save enough money to build a new house. And if sometimes, just sometimes, he hated his job - well, it couldn't be helped. The seals were so beautiful, round-eyed and funny. Their songs swelled and soared with the swish of the waves. But he hardened his heart. His family came first, no matter what happened.

One morning, he went to the strand as usual. A seal lay sleeping on rocks by the shore.

'This is a big one, he'll make lots of money,' Hamish said to himself. Creeping up silently, he plunged in his knife. With a cry, the seal slipped into the sea, sliding under the waves with the knife in his side. Hamish was annoyed.

'There goes my best knife,' he thought. 'I'll have to use the smaller one until next week's market. Time to go home anyway. There'll be no more seals today.'

He set off for home. Then, out of nowhere, a horse stood before him. On its back sat a man he had never seen before. Dressed in black from neck to ankle, he was strangely handsome.

'Are you the seal catcher?' asked the Stranger.

'I am indeed,' Hamish answered.

'I need twenty sealskins. Can you supply them?'

'Of course,' said Hamish, 'I'll have them next week.'

'That won't do, it's too late. I need them this evening.'

'The seals have gone for today; they'll be back in the morning,' said Hamish hurriedly. 'I'll have all you need by tomorrow at midday.'

'I need them this evening,' the Stranger repeated. 'I know a place where there's plenty of seals. If you climb up behind me we can get there in minutes.'

'Very well, let's get going.'

They started off, Hamish wondering where the Stranger would lead him. After all he knew every cove, every inlet, the very best places where seals came to bask.

They galloped for miles. Soon the countryside was empty of houses. Clouds gathered, trees leaned from the whip of the breeze. Nothing looked familiar.

'Here we are,' said the Stranger, as they stopped on a cliff.

Hamish dismounted and peered over the edge. There wasn't a seal to be seen, just the sea booming and thrashing the rocks. A cold feeling of dread came over him. He turned to the Stranger.

'Where are the seals you told me about?' he asked.

'You'll see them soon enough,' the Stranger answered.

Then everything happened at once. Suddenly Hamish was falling from the cliff – down, down, down into the roaring ocean. Diving beside him was the handsome Stranger.

Hamish hit the water with a smack. Waves crashed as he plunged through the blue-green gloom.

'This is the end of me,' he gasped, 'I'm sure to drown.' But to his surprise his breath came easily, no water in his lungs and no gulping for air. The Stranger dropped beside him as they sank ever deeper. Their fall only ended when they reached the sea floor.

There stood a door, studded in seashells, opening into a wonderful cavern. Walls shimmered with seaweed, sand sparkled on the floor. Coral and pearls hung in pink and blue clusters. Fish hovered and darted in brilliant shoals.

He turned to the Stranger, wondering what was happening. But no question came. The Stranger was a man no longer, but a sleek seal. He swam away, leaving Hamish alone with the others. Only then did he notice his own skin and flippers – he too was now a seal!

'Oh, no!' he thought. 'What's become of me? I should have paid heed to the legend. This is my punishment - I'll be a seal forever!' He almost sobbed at the thought of this curse. Around him groups of seals swam to and fro. He couldn't help noticing that they looked upset. Some were sighing, some sobbing, some wiping their eyes. He wondered what had happened. Poor creatures! Why were they so sad and distressed? Then the Stranger returned with a long, sharp knife. Hamish almost lost his courage.

'They're going to kill me!' he thought. 'They're getting their revenge. I'll never see my family again.'

'Is this your property?' asked the Stranger, as he held up the knife.

Hamish gasped and backed away. It was indeed his hunting knife, bent and blood-stained, the one he'd used that morning on the sleeping seal. Miserably he nodded.

'I'm sorry,' he cried, 'please, forgive me!' He closed his eyes - surely now his last moment had come. But the seals swam gently round him and nudged him with their noses.

'We mean no harm,' they said. 'We will not hurt you. But please, if you can help us, we'll be forever grateful.'

'Anything!' cried Hamish. 'I'll do anything in my power to make up for what I've done.'

'Then come with me,' said the Stranger. Hamish followed him to a smaller cave. An old seal lay on a bed of seaweed, his side ripped open in a jagged gash.

'This is my father,' said the Stranger. 'This morning you wounded him. He is a selkie like me – sometimes seal, sometimes human. Mostly, however, we live in the ocean. I brought you here to heal him. Only the one who hurts a seal can make him well again.'

'I know little about healing,' said Hamish humbly, 'but I'll do my best. I beg your pardon for the injury I have caused.'

Carefully he washed the selkie's wound and bound it with seaweed. The old selkie sighed and stretched. Then rolling off his bed, he swam back to the others. Clapping and cheering the seals came up beside him, touching him gently with their noses and flippers. Hamish stayed alone in the shadows. His heart was heavy as he looked around. What would become of him now?

The Stranger swam up to him.

'You are free to go,' he said, 'but on one condition.'

Hamish almost leaped for joy.

'Anything!' he said. 'Just tell me what you want.'

'You must promise never to hunt or kill a seal again.'

'I promise! I promise with all my heart. I will never hunt a seal again as long as I live. I will care for and protect them for the rest of my life.'

'And I will,' he thought, 'I'll find some other job. The seals will be safe as long as I live.'

Seconds later, his head was over water. He was human again! Beside him swam the Stranger. Hamish gasped and gulped with all his might. How wonderful to breathe fresh air, to taste salt, to feel the sun! Even the screaming seagulls seemed musical.

They swam ashore and climbed to the cliff top, the horse still grazing where they'd left him. Setting off at a gallop, they soon reached the cottage gate.

'Thank you for bringing me safely home,' said Hamish. 'I will keep my promise. I will never hunt a seal again.'

The Stranger reached into his saddlebag and pulled out a sack. He handed it to Hamish.

'You will never want for anything by keeping your promise,' he said. Then turning his horse he rode down towards the shore. Hamish watched till he was out of sight.

When Hamish went into the kitchen, everyone was home. They gazed in astonishment as he opened the sack, pouring gold coins across the floor. As they crowded around he told them his adventure.

They counted the coins over and over. And yes, there was more than enough for a lifetime – for Grandfather and Grandmother, for Father and Mother, for three sisters, two brothers, a cousin and a baby – and for Hamish himself, of course.

The Stranger never returned. The seals still came to bask on the rocks. They were so beautiful, round-eyed and funny. Hamish often thought of their underwater world, but it was no place for him. He never hunted seals any more but told his story wherever he went.

★ ★ ★

If ever you go to the north of Scotland – and I hope you do – you will find people there who still tell this tale. And if you're lucky, you might see the selkies for yourself.

BLAANID'S SECRET

A story from the Isle of Man

Manus flung open the curtains as the sun rose.

'Get up, Blaanid, I'm off to work,' he said.

'It's much too early,' yawned Blaanid, 'and besides, I'm so sleepy.'

'The floor needs sweeping, there's washing to be done,' Manus said. 'You know I have to hurry to get in the harvest. I haven't time to work in the house today. And when are you going to buy wool for the spinning?'

'*Traa go leor*, time enough,' she said, turning over in the bed.

'Blaanid,' he said, 'I wish I could stay at home to help but there's rain on the way. I need to get the oats stacked.' He reached for his jacket. 'See, my jacket's threadbare. It won't last another winter. I need you to spin the wool for the weaver.'

'You know I can't spin,' murmured Blaanid, pulling the blankets over her head.

'Then it's time you learned!' Manus snapped. 'I'll buy the wool myself this very day. The sooner you start, the sooner it's done.'

There was no answer from the bed.

Manus and Blaanid lived at the foot of Cronk ny Arrey Laa. The valley houses were all much the same. Floors were swept, windows washed, fires burned cheerily on hearths. Every day, spinning wheels hummed in the kitchens. The weaver's loom clattered, weaving cloth for his neighbours.

Manus's house, though, was not like the rest. True, it was freshly whitewashed outside, with neat straw ropes holding down the thatch. It was a different story on the inside. Cobwebs hung from the rafters, dust rested on clutter. Ashes dirtied the hearth, mugs stood unwashed on the dresser. As for the spinning

wheel, it stayed in the corner. For Blaanid, housework was too much bother. As for spinning – all that carding and rolling before you even start! It was out of the question. It was much more interesting to visit the neighbours, looking for news and listening to gossip

'I'm an unfortunate man,' thought Manus, as he set off for the fields. 'Here I am with a wife who won't work, a house that's filthy and my jacket in tatters. I have to save the oats, milk the cows, and clean out the stables. I'm working outside from dawn till dusk – I can't do everything. Something must be done.' He felt crosser and crosser as he gathered the oats and tied them into stooks.

'Soon the weather will turn cold. The potatoes must be dug and the wind will be bitter. I need a new jacket and that's all about it,' he said to himself.

Down the path there went Blaanid, off to visit the neighbours.

'Right!' he thought, as he straightened himself up. 'Tonight things will be different.'

In the evening no supper waited on the table. The fire was out and Blaanid sat dozing on the settle. Manus flung a sack at her feet.

'Here's the wool for my jacket,' he said. 'You have a month to spin it.'

'*Traa go leor,*' answered Blaanid, yawning and stretching. 'Any news?'

Manus thumped the table till the dishes rattled.

'Now listen to me!' he yelled. 'I've had enough of this. I need a new jacket and that's that! You have one month to spin this wool for the weaver.'

Blaanid had never seen her husband so angry. Sometimes he complained about her cooking and housework. But this was the first time he'd shouted at her.

'Very well, Manus,' she said meekly, 'I'll begin tomorrow.'

Next day Blaanid got up early. She pulled out the spinning wheel and dusted it off. But the sun was shining and there was visiting to be done. After all, she had to see the Corkills' new baby. And old Catreena had cousins staying, all the way from Lancashire. They were sure to have news. Besides, it was lonely in the house by herself. She pulled on her muslin cap and latched the door behind her.

The day passed quickly. Blaanid saw the Corkills' new baby and Catreena's cousins from Lancashire. She sat in neighbours' kitchens and had tea with homemade cake, while they cooked and cleaned or ironed the sheets. They didn't have much time to talk, and she didn't offer to help. She got home just as Manus came up the path. Pushing the spinning wheel out of sight, she opened the sack. She flung some scraps of wool on the floor, sweeping them up as he lifted the latch.

'I'm glad to see you've been busy,' he said.

But the clothes weren't washed and the hens clucked hungrily at the door.

'I hadn't time to do much else,' explained Blaanid, as she went to feed them. And that was the truth, she thought to herself.

So it went on, day after day. Each evening Blaanid threw some wool on the floor. She swept it up again as Manus came home. When three weeks had passed, only one skein was done. It was coarse as thistles, knotted and tough.

'You must be almost finished spinning,' said Manus one day. 'How many skeins have you spun?'

'I'm not sure,' said Blaanid. 'They're up in the loft.'

'Why don't we count them, then?'

Blaanid thought quickly.

'Very well, I'll throw them down one by one. You can toss them back up to me as you count.'

She went up in the loft and threw down the finished skein. When Manus tossed it back, she flung it down again. Over and over she threw it, not stopping till he'd counted forty-one.

'That's all there is,' she said, 'that's the last one.'

'Well done, Blaanid,' said Manus, as he tossed it back up. 'There's plenty here for a fine, warm jacket. I'll take them to the weaver in the next few days. I knew you could do it if only you tried.' And he gave her a hug as she came down the steps.

Blaanid didn't sleep for hours. What on earth would she do? She could never spin the wool in time, not if she worked from morning till night. What would happen then? Her husband would be furious. And if the neighbours heard, she would be disgraced. Worst of all, she had no one to blame but herself.

It was then that she thought of the Giant. He lived by himself up on Cronk ny Arrey Laa. Nobody knew his name. People said he was a master spinner and a powerful worker. Everyone was afraid of him though, and kept well away.

'He's my only chance,' thought Blaanid. 'I'll visit him tomorrow.' She fell asleep as she made her plans.

She didn't sleep for long. When Manus set off for work she was up and dressed. Soon she was on the road, the sack of wool on her back. Already the leaves were starting to fall. They floated around her as she headed up the track, going higher and higher into rushes and rocks. Soon the path petered out, till nothing but mountains and boulders surrounded her.

When she thought she could go no further she turned a corner - and there before her stood the Giant's castle. It soared to the sky, so high that the top was smothered in clouds. What now? thought Blaanid. Suppose he throws me in the dungeon, or eats me for lunch? But there was no going back. With trembling hand, she knocked at the door.

'Who is it? Who is it?' a voice roared.

'It–it–it's Blaanid fr–fr–from the valley,' she stuttered.

She pushed open the door. The Giant before her stood thirty feet tall. His hair hung in tatters, he was thin as a rope. Around him stood dozens and dozens of spinning wheels. Skeins of all colours hung from the rafters, spilling in rainbows over the floor.

'What do you want?' asked the Giant, 'I'm not fond of visitors.'

'I–I–I need your help,' Blaanid stammered, as she told him her problem.

'Ha, ha!' laughed the Giant, 'what a story, what a story! I'll spin your wool surely but only for fun.'

'For fun?' asked Blaanid, puzzled.

'What's my name?' the Giant asked, 'Can you tell me my name?'

'I don't know, I'm afraid – is Mr Giant ok?'

'Mr Giant, Mr Giant indeed! Come back in three days. The yarn shall be yours if you tell me my name. That's the bargain – your yarn if you tell me my name.'

'Very well,' Blaanid said, 'I'll know your name by then.'

With a much lighter heart, Blaanid scrambled back down the track.

'Someone surely knows his name,' she thought. 'I'll enquire from the neighbours and houses I visit.'

Next day when Manus left, she set off on her travels. From house to house she travelled with only one question:

'What's the name of the Giant who lives on Cronk ny Arrey Laa?'

But though people made suggestions, no one knew for certain. Some guessed and others thought that his name was this or that. Next day was the same. She walked further and further, asking neighbour and stranger. Always the answer was the same:

'Sorry, I don't know.'

Tired and footsore she went home in the evening; she'd never walked so far in her life. She thought about Manus – how weary he must be after such long days, how tired after working for hours in the fields. So she swept up the floor and dusted the dresser.

That evening, Manus was late home. Blaanid lit the lamp. She stirred up the fire to warm his supper. When at last he returned, he ate every scrap.

'That was lovely, Blaanid,' he said, 'and you've tidied the house. The day after tomorrow, I'll go to the weaver. I'll be ready for winter, all thanks to my good wife.'

Blaanid felt like crying. Tomorrow she had to collect the yarn, but she still didn't know the Giant's name. He would never give it to her. And what would become of her then?

'You're very quiet, Blaanid,' said Manus. 'Don't you want to hear my news?'

'Of course!' Blaanid answered, as she wiped the table. She couldn't let him see her tears.

'You won't believe what happened today. I had to go across the mountains on business. This evening coming back, I passed the Giant's castle.'

He paused for a moment.

'You spin very well, my dear, but the Giant is even better.'

'What do you mean?' whispered Blaanid, almost afraid to ask.

'The window was open, so I thought I'd peep in. His hands whirled like the wind, so fast you couldn't see them. Three spinning wheels spun together as he dashed from one to the other. He was laughing and cheering, singing over and over:

> 'Spin, wheels, spin;
>
> Spin fast or spin slow.
>
> The wool is hers, the yarn is mine,
>
> For she will never know
>
> That Mollyndroat is my name.
>
> That's the end of the guessing-game.'

Blaanid almost fainted for joy.

'What a funny song!' she exclaimed. 'Sing it to me again.'

Manus laughed and sang it again. The third time, Blaanid joined in. The fourth time she sang it by herself. And if Manus had woken in the night he would have heard her singing it still.

As soon as he was gone next morning, she set off for the mountain. The weather had changed. Mist soaked through her clothes, her feet slithered and slipped. Shivering with cold, she pulled her shawl round her.

'Poor Manus,' she thought, as she struggled up the track. 'I can stay indoors by the fire all winter, while he has to slave outside in the rain. He needs a warm jacket.'

To keep her spirits up, she started to sing:

> 'Spin, wheels, spin;
>
> Spin fast or spin slow.
>
> The wool is mine, the yarn is mine,
>
> And all because I know
>
> That Mollyndroat is his name
>
> And that's the end of the guessing-game.'

When at last she reached the castle, she knocked boldly on the door.

'I've come for my yarn,' she said, as she pushed it open.

The Giant sat surrounded by balls of wool.

'So you have,' he said, 'but first tell me my name.'

Blaanid pretended not to know.

'Is it Mollynrea?' she asked.

'It is not,' replied the Giant.

'Then it's Mollynruiy,' she declared.

'Not that either,' grinned the Giant.

'I know! It's Mollynchreest!'

'Wrong again!' the Giant laughed.

Blaanid kept guessing, while the Giant juggled the balls of wool in the air.

'One more guess,' he said at last, 'then be off – I've had enough of this. A bargain's a bargain.'

Then Blaanid straightened her shoulders and began to sing:

> 'Spin, wheels, spin;
>
> Spin fast or spin slow.
>
> The wool is mine, the yarn is mine,
>
> And all because I know

That Mollyndroat is your name

And that's the end of the guessing-game!'

When the Giant heard this, he roared with rage.

'Who told you this? I'll tear him to pieces! I'll chop off his head!'

'A bargain's a bargain,' said Blaanid, 'now give me my yarn.'

'You cheated! You cheated!'

Mollyndroat bellowed so loudly that the windows rattled. People shuddered in the valley to hear such thunder.

'My yarn, if you please,' said Blaanid, though her teeth chattered.

Screaming and cursing he hurled the balls at her. She just had time to gather them up before he slammed the door.

That evening when Manus came home, the house was spotless. The stew was delicious, the apple-tart even better. A basket full of smooth, blue yarn stood waiting on the dresser. Manus sighed with contentment.

'Tomorrow I'll visit the weaver. What a lucky man I am – a wonderful wife, a beautiful home and a warm jacket for the winter!'

★ ★ ★

In the valley by Cronk ny Arrey Laa, all the houses are much the same. Floors are swept, windows washed, fires burn cheerily on hearths. Did Blaanid learn to spin? I don't know. But whenever you go there, you can ask her for yourself.

THE MAGIC PAIL

A story from Cornwall

Once long ago, on the wild moors of Cornwall, lived a man and his wife. Their cottage stood in a nook miles from the nearest house. On the rooftop lay a row of tiles carved in pretty patterns. They were dainty and neat – and perfect for fairy dancers. Or so Jenny believed.

All day she sat in the house while Jack worked at the mines. Because she was crippled she could not go out. She spent her time watching for the 'Small People' to pass. She said she heard them whispering in the grass.

'It's only the wind rustling in the heather,' Jack told her, though he did not argue. If only she had a baby to care for! But no baby came and her days were empty and long.

One stormy November evening, something fumbled at the door. Jenny looked at the clock.

'Jack's home early,' she thought.

The door creaked open. She stared in astonishment as a tiny woman stepped in, muffled in the oddest bonnet and cloak. The basket she carried was covered in leaves. Placing it on the floor she started to sing:

> 'I bring you my dear, till the time of that year
>
> when the spell shall be broken, and this is the token-
>
> the magic of pail and the wail of the hare.
>
> But sometimes it's better
>
> to give back a treasure.
>
> So listen to this, remember and hear.'

A puff of smoke gushed down the chimney and she was gone. Jenny sat speechless. Though she believed in fairies, she'd never expected to see one in

her own kitchen.

Just then, Jack returned from work.

'Let's see what's in the basket,' he said, when he heard.

Brushing aside the leaves they looked in. There soundly sleeping, lay the smallest, ugliest baby they had ever seen.

'By all that's holy!' Jack exclaimed, 'that's no human creature! I'll leave it out on the moor this very minute!'

'Leave it out on the moor? On a night like this?' retorted Jenny. 'I don't care what it is, no living creature is going out in this storm. I'll look after the little thing myself, and we'll see what morning brings.'

Jenny refused to go to bed. All night she sat up, though the creature never stirred. As daylight dawned, the wind died down. Jack stoked up the fire.

'The storm is over. I'll leave that basket out by the cairn,' he said, glancing in. Just then the creature opened its eyes and smiled up at him. The thin face looked almost beautiful. Delighted, Jack smiled back.

'Maybe we'll wait until evening', he said.

'Maybe we will,' Jenny agreed.

How fast the day went! There was so much to tell Jack when he came home – that the little creature was a girl, that her clothes were of the finest lace, that hidden under the covers was a polished pail. Round the rim was writing that neither one could read. Jack left it on the dresser where it glowed honey-gold.

'It must be a toy,' he thought, 'but what a strange one.'

Of course the child stayed. They named her Tamsyn. As she got older she grew clever and quick. Jenny taught her to sew and cook and bake. Like any child, she was sometimes naughty. Then a strange thing happened – the pail on the dresser grew plain and dull. But as soon as she behaved, it sparkled again.

No one could say that Tamsyn was pretty. Though her hair was fair, her face stayed sharp and thin. But her dark eyes were bright with mischief; she ran and danced about the house till Jenny was quite dizzy. She grew only a little, no taller than the fire tongs. She was so tiny that Jenny was afraid to let her out.

Then spring came and brought with it chicks and cowslips. Tamsyn grew restless.

'Please let me go outside, just for a while,' she begged. 'I want to shout and jump and run!'

Jack was getting ready for work.

'She can walk some of the road with me,' he said.

So Tamsyn skipped along beside him, asking questions and talking all the time.

'That's far enough, little one,' he said when the mines were in sight. 'Now go straight back home.'

Tamsyn promised to go home at once and Jack continued on.

When he returned that evening, Jenny was frantic. Tamsyn hadn't come home. Crazy with worry, Jack dashed back outside. Shouting and calling he found her at last, sitting in heather a mile from the house.

'I got lost,' she said. 'A big hare with long ears would not let me pass. Then a kind lady chased him. She said I must never go out without the pail.'

After that, Tamsyn had to stay at home. For years she was only allowed play in the garden. It was so boring.

'I'm so tired of the garden,' she said one morning, 'and besides, now I'm ten I can look after myself.'

'Very well,' said Jenny at last, 'but you must be very careful and be back by noon.'

Tamsyn was delighted. Climbing on the stool, she took the pail from the dresser.

'What shall I bring you home in the pail, Mammy?' she asked.

'A bucketful of the skylark's song,' said Jenny, smiling.

It was spring again and lovely for rambling. Rabbits played, gorse bloomed, skylarks swooped and sang.

Just before noon she dashed in, breathless.

'Long Ears the Hare tried to catch me,' she said, 'but he ran away when I rattled the pail.'

That evening, as Jenny sat knitting, music pealed around the kitchen.

'Oh!' gasped Jenny, 'Oh! What is it? Who's singing?'

'It's the skylark, Mammy,' Tamsyn said. 'I brought his song home in the pail.'

It was the sweetest music Jenny had heard in years. Closing her eyes she leaned back to listen. On and on went the singing, filling the room, spilling out trills. Then something went 'scritch, scratch, scritch' at the window.

'It's a skylark!' said Tamsyn, opening it wide.

'Give me back my song,' begged the skylark, 'I can't live without it.'

Annoyed, Jenny opened her eyes.

'Be off with you! Your song is mine now!' she said crossly.

'Mammy,' said Tamsyn, 'if we keep the skylark's song he won't find a mate. There'll be no baby skylarks next year.'

Then Jenny remembered what the tiny woman had said –

'– sometimes it's better
to give back a treasure.'

'You're right, Tamsyn,' she said. 'I'm a foolish, selfish woman. Give the lark back his song.'

As the pail emptied, the lark took flight, soaring and singing away into the evening.

For weeks Tamsyn wandered on the moor. Everywhere she went she brought the pail. But one morning it began to rain. For hours and hours, rain splashed down the gutters. Soon garden and moor were muddy and puddled.

'You must stay inside, Tamsyn,' Jenny said. 'It's easy to catch cold in this wet weather.'

So Tamsyn stayed indoors, playing with the kittens and helping in the house.

In a few weeks the rain stopped.

'Please, Mammy, let me out on the moor,' said Tamsyn. 'The sun's shining and I'm tired of being inside.'

'Very well,' Jenny agreed, 'but you must be home by noon.'

Tamsyn ran to fetch the pail.

'What shall I bring you home today, Mammy?' she asked.

'A bucketful of sunbeams,' Jenny said. She could see them shining on the pool by the cairn.

Tamsyn was excited to be outdoors again. Summer had come. Cuckoos called, bluebells bloomed, pools were thick with frogspawn.

Just before noon she dashed in, breathless.

'Long Ears the Hare tried to catch me,' she said 'but he ran away when I rattled the pail.'

That evening as Jenny sat sewing, a wonderful light filled the kitchen. Rays poured golden from corner to corner. Jenny had never seen anything so glorious. She clapped her hands in delight.

'What is it? Oh, what is it?' she cried.

'It's the sunbeams from the pool,' Tamsyn answered. 'I brought them home in the pail.'

They watched as the sunbeams danced across the ceiling, shining on the jugs and plates on the dresser. But what was that gurgling noise? Tamsyn opened the door. There on the doorstep lay a pool of dull water.

'Give me back my sunbeams,' the water begged, 'I can't shine without them and all my light is gone.'

But Jenny was annoyed.

'Be off with you! Your sunbeams are mine now!' she said crossly.

'Mammy,' said Tamsyn, 'if we keep the sunbeams, the pool will lose its light.

Everything in it will shrivel and die.'

Then Jenny remembered what the tiny woman had sung:

'– sometimes it's better

to give back a treasure.'

'You're right, Tamsyn,' she said. 'I'm a foolish, selfish woman. Give the pool back its sunbeams.'

Tamsyn poured the sunbeams out on the water. Glittering like sequins it trickled off home.

One morning orange leaves blew in on the floor.

'Autumn already!' Jenny exclaimed.

'What shall I bring home in my pail today, Mammy?' asked Tamsyn.

'Bring me that hare that bothers you so much,' Jenny said.

For hours Tamsyn wandered the moor. Haws reddened the hedgerows, there were blackberries and rosehips.

Suddenly, Long Ears hopped from behind a rock. Startled, Tamsyn backed away. Then she remembered what her Mammy had asked for.

'Come here, Mr Long Ears,' she called. 'Come and see what's in the pail.'

She couldn't help shivering as the hare hopped nearer.

'See, Long Ears, see the lovely pail. Guess what's hidden inside.'

The hare came closer. Tamsyn whispered and coaxed till he could resist no longer. As soon as he hopped in, the pail made him prisoner. Just to be sure, Tamsyn tied it down with her apron.

Jenny saw her anxious face as she ran in the door.

'It's the hare! I caught Long Ears, just as you told me.'

Jenny snatched the pail and tied the apron tighter. The hare bounced and leaped inside, trying to escape.

'Well done, Tamsyn,' she said. 'We'll leave him there. He deserves to be punished for all the times he scared you.'

Later, when she'd finished baking, Jenny looked in the pail. The hare stared up at her with huge, frightened eyes. He looked so scared that she felt sorry for him.

'Don't be one bit sorry,' Tamsyn said. 'He's really a hobgoblin in disguise. Once he was cruel to a fairy baby. Her mother had to hide her to keep her safe.'

'How do you know that?' asked Jenny in wonder.

'The 'Small People' told me when I was sleeping,' she replied.

All at once something scrabbled at the door. Four baby hares crouched on the doorstep.

'Give us back our Daddy Long Ears!' they wailed. 'Daddy, Daddy, come home, come home!'

Long Ears began to plead and cry.

'Please let me go!' he begged. 'Please let me go home to my children!'

'Daddy Long Ears, Daddy Long Ears, come home, come home!' the little hares screeched. In the middle of the racket, Jack came back from work.

'I think we should make a nice Hare Hot-pot,' Jack said. 'Then Mr Long Ears will bother us no more.'

At once the hare started howling and screaming. The baby hares bawled, calling for their Daddy. Tamsyn began to feel sorry for them all.

'The baby hares are so upset,' she said. 'We could set Long Ears free if he swears to go away.'

'Let's see what Mr Hare has to say,' Jack said.

He glared at the hare huddled in the pail.

'Do you promise to leave these moors at once?'

'I do, oh I DO!' the hare whimpered.

'Then, in the name of Tamsyn, I order you to go away. You must not return for five hundred years. If you do, we will make you into a meat pasty.'

Long Ears screamed in terror.

'I promise! I promise I won't return for five hundred years,' he squealed.

'Then off you go,' Jack ordered, 'and remember what I said!' He tipped the pail out on the doorstep. The hare darted across the moor with the small hares scrambling after.

Every morning after that Tamsyn walked to the mines. And though the hare had gone away, she always brought the pail.

One November morning, when Tamsyn looked out, the sky was heavy and dull. Everything was silent and still.

'This will be our last walk for a while,' said Jack. 'It's going to snow; you might lose your way and get lost in a snow-drift.'

'What shall I bring you home in the pail today, Mammy?' Tamsyn asked, as she put on her boots.

'Bring me your own self,' Jenny answered with a laugh.

Muffled against the frost, they started off. Ice crackled in puddles, wild geese honked above their heads. As they walked, Jack noticed that Tamsyn was very quiet. She didn't ask any questions and she didn't hop or skip. He was troubled by her silence.

'That's far enough, little one,' he said when they neared the mines. 'Tell me, what did Mammy ask you for today?'

'She asked me for my own self,' Tamsyn answered, 'but I'm not sure I can do that.'

As he turned to go he heard her talking to herself.

'Tamsyn, give me yourself,' she muttered, 'Tamsyn, give me yourself.'

To his astonishment she jumped in the pail and clattered back towards the cottage.

Jenny was surprised when the pail bounced in the door. There was Tamsyn inside, looking up at her.

'See, Mammy, I've brought you myself,' she said. 'Please give me back my own self.'

'I give you back your own self. Now come out at once, you little goose! Why did you jump in the pail?'

'Because you asked me to bring back my own self.' Tamsyn put the pail back on the dresser. 'But I don't know who myself is,' she whispered.

They spent the evening patching a quilt. Tamsyn hardly spoke. She asked to go to bed early – she still slept in the basket near the hearth. Jenny was worried. Was the child ill? At suppertime she peeped in to check. Startled, she called Jack. Together they looked into the tiny bed. There lay Tamsyn as they'd never seen her before. She was beautiful – hair cloudy gold, skin pearly and pink. Lace fine as cobwebs covered her over, while tucked in a corner was the magic pail.

Before they could speak, the door creaked open. There stood the tiny woman from ten years before. Stepping across the floor, she looked in the basket. In her high, squeaky voice she started to sing:

'Give me my Tamsyn, my dear little daughter.

The time is now up, we'll feast and we'll sup

in the cairn till morning,

 so give me my darling…'

Jenny screamed in horror.

'I can't give Tamsyn back!' she cried. 'Please don't ask me, please, please! I'll give you anything you ask for, but not her, please. Please, not her!'

Then Tamsyn opened her eyes. She didn't say a word, but looked up at Jenny. And Jenny remembered the skylark, the sunbeams and the hare. She remembered too that

'– sometimes it's better

to give back a treasure.'

Tears streamed down her face as she spoke:

'I'm a foolish, selfish woman,' she sobbed. 'Take her, though she's indeed my dearest treasure. Take Tamsyn, and thank you for lending her to us for ten happy years.'

Picking up the basket, the tiny woman sang once more:

'And so it's goodbye, till a birdie may fly

to its own precious nest, to the heart that's true

to the one who knew

 it's better to give

than to keep for oneself.'

She left them standing there alone. Through the open door, Jenny saw hundreds of 'Small People' coming across the moor, singing and dancing and waving scarlet stars. They lit the way, till the tiny woman and her basket disappeared into the cairn …

★ ★ ★

For several months, Jenny and Jack were heartbroken. Jack still went every day to the mines. Jenny watched for the 'Small People' passing. Sometimes she thought she saw Tamsyn, or heard her laugh.

'It's only the wind rustling in the heather,' Jack told her, though he did not argue.

But soon Jenny's days were busy again. Before winter came round once more, Jenny and Jack had a baby of their own. And though they loved this little girl with all their hearts, they never forgot Tamsyn – the fairy child who stayed with them for ten happy years.

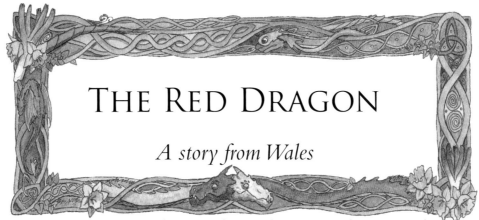

THE RED DRAGON

A story from Wales

Long ago, ages before you and I were born, there was a boy named Huw.
His mother was a widow so he helped her all he could. They lived in a valley
surrounded by mountains. Few people came to visit since the place was so
remote, and nothing ever happened there. And though Huw worked willingly,
he longed for adventure.

One day, a wandering beggar came to the door. He brought unwelcome
news. The king, Gwrtheyrn, had been defeated in battle. Saxon invaders had
beaten his army and the whole kingdom was in dreadful danger.

'The king will need every man he can get,' said the beggar.

'I would gladly go to fight,' Huw thought, as he lay in bed that night, 'but my
mother needs me. There's no one else to help her with the work.'

★ ★ ★

Meanwhile, back at the court, King Gwrtheyrn was depressed. What should he
do? The Saxons were stronger than anyone had suspected. How could he save
his kingdom? He called together his twelve wisest men.

'Tell me what to do,' he begged, 'to keep the Saxons out.'

'You must build a fortress on the hill,' the wise men told him. 'Our soldiers
will keep guard. They will see the enemy coming and be prepared to fight.'

The king thought this was good advice. He gave orders at once for the
fortress to be built. Every man who could hold a shovel was summoned to the
site. Work began early next morning. The valleys rang with the clang of metal
on stone. All day the men worked, scarcely pausing for food or rest. In the

evening, the king came to inspect.

'The Saxon enemy may come at any time,' he told the workmen. 'You must work harder. I will richly reward the fastest worker.'

The men trudged home, each determined to claim the reward. They returned next day eager to begin. But a shock awaited them. Every trench was filled – nothing remained of their work but scattered soil and stones.

King Gwrtheyrn was furious.

'The Saxon enemy has tricked us!' he shouted. 'Today you must work faster than ever. Tonight our sentries will stand guard.'

The men worked through the summer heat. Mealtimes came and went but nobody stopped to rest. They ate and drank where they stood, sweat dripping, backs aching. By evening the foundations were finished. The exhausted men dropped their tools where they fell and headed home. Twenty sentries were left on guard.

'No Saxon fiend will fool us this time!' King Gwrtheyrn declared.

Next day as dawn broke, the workmen returned. The sentries yawned and stretched, looking forward to a good sleep. Then a shout went up.

'My hammer! Where's my hammer?' a man called out.

'My axe! Who took my axe?' another yelled.

And so it went on, as each man searched for his missing tools. Not one was left.

'Those stupid sentries fell asleep,' roared the king. 'Throw them in the dungeon!'

'But your Majesty!' cried the sentries. 'We watched all night and nothing stirred, neither bat nor badger.'

The king paid no attention but had them flung in the dungeon. Every blacksmith in the land made new sets of tools. Soon the men were working even harder. Anyone who paused to rest would be severely punished.

Three evenings later, the walls were half built. The workers collected their tools and dragged themselves home. Fifty sentries were put on guard. All night they marched round and round the fortress. They did not want to end up in the dungeon.

But as the sun came up, they stared about in horror …

One unlucky sentry was sent to tell the king.

'Your Ma–Ma–Majesty, it's ha–ha–ha–happened again. All the walls were smashed in the night.'

'What!' The king leaped to his feet. When he reached the site, all was in chaos. Walls lay tumbled left and right, not a stone was left upon a stone.

'Those stupid sentries fell asleep!' roared the king. 'Throw them in the dungeon!'

'But your Majesty,' cried the sentries, 'we watched all night and nothing stirred, neither branch nor bramble.'

'To the dungeon!' screamed the king.

The sentries were hustled away while the workmen stood speechless.

Distraught, King Gwrtheyrn called his twelve wise men.

'What can be happening?' he demanded. 'Are our enemies invisible?'

'No, your Majesty,' they answered. 'There is, however, an evil spirit in this place. We need a sacrifice to keep him from harming us.'

'A sacrifice? What sacrifice?' There was silence for a moment.

'It must be a young boy,' mumbled one wise man at last, 'a boy without a father.'

'Then search the kingdom!' cried the king. 'He who brings back such a boy will be well rewarded.'

The wise men were troubled. How could the king do such a thing? Yet they must save the kingdom …

'The boy must be honoured,' they said. 'His sacrifice should be remembered, his family rewarded.'

'Yes, yes, yes – whatever you say,' snapped the king. 'Just find him as soon as possible and bring him here.'

The news spread quickly. Some left their farms and forges to go searching. Others hugged their children and kept them hidden. What if the right boy could not be found? If so, any child might be chosen. Doors were locked and bolted, neighbours stopped visiting. For Huw and his mother, life went on as normal. The awful news had not yet reached the valley.

★ ★ ★

One of the searchers was named Dafydd. He worked in the stables, cleaning and sweeping. It was a job he hated. How he longed for the king's gold! If only he were successful, he would never shovel horse-dung again. He set off at once, trudging through the countryside for days and days. He didn't see a single child – they were all safely indoors.

One evening, tired and footsore, he came to a valley. A wild, remote place, it was surrounded by mountains. As he began to make camp, he heard children shouting. He looked around to see four boys fighting, three against one. Dafydd thought this unfair and went to separate them.

'Stop this at once!' he said, pulling them apart. One boy lay on the ground, clothes torn, nose bleeding. He looked up at Dafydd with dark, fearless eyes.

'Why are there three against one?' Dafydd asked the boy. 'What mischief have you done?'

The boy got to his feet, wiping his nose and face.

'I told them I have special powers but they don't believe me.' He brushed the dust off his tunic. 'They were fighting with me because I have no father to protect me,' he continued. 'He died before I was born.'

Dafydd could barely hide his joy.

'Come with me,' he said. 'The king has need of a boy such as you.'

53

Huw was delighted.

'First I must tell my mother,' he said. 'Then I will come with you.'

When his mother heard she was pleased for her son, but also a bit worried.

'The king lives so far away,' she said, as she prepared supper. 'I hope you won't be gone for long. Soon the oats will be ready and I'll need you for the harvest.' She paused and looked at him. 'I'll miss you, Huw. You're all I have in the world.'

'Don't worry, mother, I'll be back before the next full moon. Besides, it's such an honour,' said Huw. Then, hugging her quickly, he set off with Dafyyd.

Huw thought it a great adventure as they set out on their travels. Hills, valleys and forests were bursting with summer. Grasses swayed in the breeze, poppies bloomed, bees lingered in the heat. But at last they came to their journey's end. Huw was excited – what task would he have to do, he wondered.

'This is the boy you were looking for,' Dafydd said when they stood before the king. 'His father died before he was born. Now give me the gold if you please, your Majesty.'

'He shall be sacrificed at once,' the king said. 'Then you shall have your reward.'

Huw turned pale. Sacrificed? That meant he would be killed! Was this his punishment for fighting? He hadn't started the fight, and what about the other boys? He might never see his mother again. But he held his head high as he asked the king to explain.

When he heard the king's tale he was silent. Was this the time to test his special powers? There was no-one to help him; he must rely on himself.

'Your Majesty,' Huw said at last, 'may I at least speak to the men who advised you?'

'Very well,' said the king crossly, 'but you must prepare to die.'

By the time the wise men entered, a crowd had gathered. All had heard that a boy was to be sacrificed. They could scarcely believe it. How could the king be so cruel?

Huw questioned the twelve men.

'What lies under the ground where the fortress is being built?'

The wise men discussed this together but they couldn't answer.

'I will tell you,' said Huw. 'There is a lake under the ground. If you dig deep enough you will find it.'

The king looked at the boy properly for the first time. There was something about him that made him listen.

'Have the workmen dig deeply,' he commanded, 'and see if the boy is right.'

No sooner said than done. An hour later the first sign of water appeared. To everyone's surprise it opened out into a lake. Huw turned to the wise men again.

'What is in the lake?' he asked. The wise men shrugged their shoulders.

'I will tell you. There are two caves, one to the east and another to the west. Please, your Majesty, send your men to find them.'

The king wondered about the boy as he gave the order, everyone waiting quietly till the men returned.

'We found the caves just as the boy said,' they reported.

The wise men were starting to look nervous as Huw faced them again.

'What lies in the caves?' he asked them. This time they didn't even answer.

'I will tell you. There is a serpent in each,' declared the boy. 'One is red and one is white. Please, your Majesty, send men to find them. But be very careful-they are getting ready to fight.'

At this, Dafydd jumped out of the crowd.

'This is nonsense!' he shouted. 'The boy is a coward; he is wasting our time. Let him be sacrificed! Then we can finish the fortress.'

'He has been right twice already,' said the king. 'If he is wrong this time he will be put to death.'

Diving into the lake, two men went to inspect the caves. The crowd waited silently. There wasn't a sound to be heard except water lapping and the wind's whisper. At last the men surfaced. Dripping and panting, they stood before the king.

'There is a white serpent in the cave to the east,' said one.

'There is a red serpent in the cave to the west,' said the other.

A loud cheer went up. The boy's courage had impressed everyone.

'Now you must all stand back,' Huw ordered. 'There will be a fierce battle between the serpents.'

He had scarcely finished speaking when the fight began. The creatures lunged at each other, writhing and twisting, lashing and hissing. Viciously they fought, first the red serpent winning, then the white. Suddenly, the red serpent snatched the white one in his jaws. Tossing his head, he dashed him against a rock. Slowly, the white serpent rolled over. He sank below the water, lifeless and still. Before the king could speak, the red serpent changed into a beautiful dragon! Flames erupted from his mouth as he roared in triumph. Everyone stared in astonishment at the wonderful creature.

'But what does it all mean?' whispered King Gwrtheyrn.

'The white serpent stands for the Saxons,' said the boy. 'The red serpent stands for our people. There will be many battles between us, but eventually we will win.'

Ashamed, Dafydd listened as Huw continued.

'The Red Dragon is our guardian. He will protect us to the end of time. Now, build your fortress near the coast, and leave the dragon to live here in peace.'

All was done as the boy suggested. The king, however, was furious with his 'wise men.' He banished them from his realm, then sent for Huw.

'You have saved my kingdom and given me courage,' he said. 'How can I reward you? Gold and silver? Precious jewels?'

'I want no riches,' the boy replied, 'I only want a promise. No human being must ever again be sacrificed in your kingdom.'

The king readily agreed, and all the people were delighted and relieved. Then Huw set off for home. It was time to help his mother with the harvest.

★ ★ ★

People say that when Huw grew up he became a magician. Wise and clever, he was known as Merlin. As for the dragon, he was never seen again. His image, however, is everywhere in King Gwrtheyrn's kingdom, or Wales as it is known today. Whenever you go there you can see it for yourself. It reminds the Welsh people of their noble heritage, and of one boy's courage.

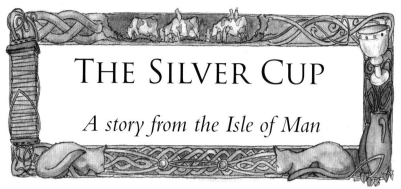

THE SILVER CUP

A story from the Isle of Man

Farmer Ned scratched his head. Something was wrong. This was the third morning in a row that his cows gave no milk. They just stood there – eyes dull, heads drooping, tails between their legs. The children came running across the yard.

'Daddy, Daddy, have you finished milking? The cats are starving.'

'The cows have no milk today,' Ned said.

'Why have the cows no milk, Daddy?'

'I wish I knew,' Ned answered.

'Maybe you should pet them while you're milking,' said the children.

'Maybe I should.'

Ned tried again, stroking the cows as he started milking. He got two fine kicks for his trouble and tumbled off the milking-stool. Margad his wife came out next.

'Ned, Ned, have you finished milking? The baby is hungry.'

'The cows have no milk again today,' said Ned, worried.

'Maybe you should play a tune for them? They say that cows love music.'

She fetched his accordion. Ned played a few tunes, feeling rather silly. But the cows just tossed their heads and mooed. Not a drop of milk in the buckets. What could be the matter?

He stood at the cow-house door, thinking. He was proud of his farm. Hens clucked in the farmyard, geese wandered past the barns. Captain, the horse, grazed in the field; the hedgerows were neat. Neighbours agreed that his was the best farm in Rushen.

'The best farm in all of the Isle of Man!' some declared.

'They wouldn't say that now,' thought Ned, 'if they could see my poor cows.'

Could it be a jealous neighbour? Had someone cast an evil spell? He had often heard tell of such things. Some even believed that 'Themselves' caused mischief. (Nobody dared to call them 'fairies'.) But weren't they old stories, told to pass long nights? He didn't believe them. Still, just to be sure, he never went near the Fairy Mound.

Ned punched the doorjamb with his fist. He would get to the bottom of this! He would find out who was stealing the cows' milk, no matter what. That night he sat looking into the fire. The children were asleep. Margad sat opposite him, spinning.

'What will we do about the cows, Ned?' she asked. 'We can't go on like this.'

Ned stood up and reached for the lantern.

'I'm going to the cow-house to keep watch,' he said. 'Somebody or something is ruining our cows. Don't wait up for me but leave a light in the window.'

'Oh, Ned, be very careful!' Margad begged. 'Who knows what happens in the dead of night!'

'Don't worry, I'll be all right. But I must find out what's going on.'

He put on his coat and lit the lantern. Wind stirred restlessly as he crossed the yard to the cow-house. All the cows were lying in their stalls. They scarcely glanced up as he quenched the lantern and burrowed under the straw.

The long wait began. An hour passed, then another and another. Draughts licked his feet, the straw tickled. Ned yawned. Stiff and sore, he shuddered with cold, thinking of the kitchen and his warm bed. He was just about to give up when he thought he heard voices. Cautiously he lifted his head. Light glimmered under the door, which slowly opened. Ned almost gasped out loud.

Droves of little men – no taller than the milking-stool – came pouring into the cow-house. Some carried torches while others held whips. Each was dressed in a green jacket. Leather caps covered their heads, while tiny hunting-

horns were strapped to their belts. They were laughing and chattering, their voices crisp as crickets.

'Hurrah!' chirped one. 'Another night gallop!'

'Poor Ned is puzzled. Human beings are so stupid.'

'Well his cows are good, anyway. Now, all aboard!'

Loosening the tethers, they leaped on the cows' backs.

'Time to go milking!' they squealed. The cows got to their feet. A few little men rode out on each beast, giggling like children as they cracked their whips.

As soon as they were gone, Ned snatched the lantern. With trembling fingers he lit the wick. Not a single cow was left. Outside, the voices were fading. Wisps of straw fluttered behind them in the breeze.

'It's "Themselves!"' Ned groaned, 'I should have guessed! But they won't get away with this! I'll follow them, if they take me to the world's end! I'll get my cows back with Captain's help.'

Without saddle or bridle, Ned leaped on Captain's back.

'Fly, my brave horse! Fly like the wind!' he shouted, as they galloped off. 'Run like you've never run before. No one steals Ned's cattle and gets away with it!'

Twigs whipped his cheeks, briars scratched his legs as they rushed over hedges and bridges and ditches. He had no idea where they were going. Grimly he clung to Captain's mane as the horse crossed a river. It wasn't long before there were lights ahead. They rose and dipped in a stream of starry sparks. Voices carried on the wind, sometimes fading and were lost. Then Ned urged Captain on harder than ever.

'Faster, Captain, faster! We must not lose them, wherever they're going!'

Just then the moon came out, and Ned saw where they were heading. It was the Fairy Mound, where no human dared venture, not even in sunniest daylight. As they neared the hill, the little men signalled with their hunting horns: 'Ta rantata rantata taaaa!'

Immediately the hillside opened, pouring golden light over boulders and bushes. As 'Themselves' rode in, Ned leaped from his horse and followed unseen.

A passage opened into a hall, arched with silver branches. Candles and lanterns cluttered the ceiling. The place was packed with little people, each one dressed in gorgeous colours. To the left were trees with leaves of purple glass. To the right a feast was being prepared. Ned watched as his cows were milked. The milk was for pancakes, the cream for wonderful desserts. Meats of all kinds were boiled and roasted, cakes and puddings and pies were baked. Juices and wines were poured into goblets.

All the while, musicians played. Crowds leaped and danced to the strange wild music, cheering and laughing in high-pitched voices. Once or twice, as the dancers whirled past, Ned thought he recognised a face. But there was no time to ask as they cantered away.

When the music ended, the dancers gathered at the tables. One whose face looked familiar whispered as he passed:

'Don't taste anything here. If you do, you'll be like me and never leave this place.'

Plates clattered, glasses chinked as the fairies feasted. There was shouting and clapping. Ned stayed in the shadows and watched. When the party was ending, the king stood up. In his hand was a glittering silver cup. He made a speech, though Ned couldn't understand a word. But he knew it was in the old Manx tongue that he had almost forgotten. The king drank first. '*Shoh slaynt!*' he cried, 'Your good health! And here's to poor, foolish Ned!' Everyone laughed as he passed the cup around. Seething, Ned looked on as each one sipped. The cup came closer. He could see that it was beautiful, jewelled with rubies and gleaming with gold. His anger grew as he watched.

'They have gold and jewels and all they could ask for, yet they stole the milk from my cows.' he thought. 'All I have is my little farm, but I'll punish their greed! I'll make them pay for my cows and milk.'

As the cup passed in front of him, he stepped into the light. Seizing it in both hands he raised it over his head.

'*Shoh slaynt!*' he cried – then tossed the wine over the whole gathering. At once the lights were quenched. All was noise and confusion. Chairs were flung over, fairies bumped into each other. They lashed out in the darkness with elbows and fists.

Ned saw a stem of light at the entrance. With cup in hand, he flung the door open, slamming it shut behind him. Not even stopping to mount his horse, he set off running. Home was miles away but he had a head start. Clutching the cup, he ran like a hare, glad of the moonlight that showed him the way.

The fairies quickly realised what had happened. Roaring with rage, they set off in pursuit. Pouring down the hill like wasps, they screamed for the human who had stolen their cup. Over his shoulder, Ned saw the mob approaching. They would soon catch up, for their powers were great. How could he trick them? He tried to remember the old stories he'd heard. Wasn't there something about water? Yes, that was it! 'Themselves' hate getting wet.

Just to the left was a field of rushes, and where there are rushes there's sure to be water. Over the fence he went, plunging and squelching. Cries of dismay rose up behind him. Still they came after him, jumping from one clump of rushes to the next. Something gleamed beyond the bushes. The river! That would save him. He leaped in, heedless of the icy cold.

'The stepping-stones! Use the stepping-stones!' a voice squealed. But Ned was too clever to fall for such a trick. He waded through the water where 'Themselves' would never venture. Soaking and frozen, he reached the opposite bank.

Nearly home now, just another mile, but the mob was getting closer. They had crossed by the stepping-stones and were catching up fast. Screaming in fury, they came charging after him. Gasping for breath, he could not run much further.

Then something loomed just ahead. It was the church tower. With one desperate spurt, he made for the churchyard. Over the stile he flew, for here he would be safe. The fairy mob howled in rage – they could not touch him in that sacred place. He leaned against the wall to catch his breath. There was Margad's candle shining in the window. And -as daylight crept over the horizon – 'Themselves' disappeared. Nothing remained but crisp, twisted leaves.

Ned made his way home. He hid the cup, changed his clothes and tumbled into bed. When he awoke it was almost midday.

'What happened last night?' asked Margad.

'I'll tell you later,' Ned said, reaching for his jacket.

He was almost afraid as he headed for the cow-house. But all the cows were home, as was his faithful Captain. He left them to rest, then showed the silver cup to his wife.

'Oh, Ned!' gasped Margad when she heard, 'what shall we do with it? Suppose "Themselves" come back? Next time they might steal the children!'

They talked for a while.

'We could sell it,' Ned said, 'it's worth a lot of money.'

'We could,' said Margad, 'but they would certainly take their revenge, and then we'd be in worse trouble.' She thought for a moment. 'As long as it's in the village, I'm sure they won't come after us. But we need to keep it in a safe place.'

Ned polished the beautiful jewels with his sleeve.

'I know!' he said. 'Let's leave it in the church!'

So that's what they did. It would be safe in St. Mary's – 'Themselves' could never enter there. Everyone was surprised when they saw it on the altar. Where had it come from? Who had left it there? Ned and Margad never said a word.

In a few days, the cows were as good as ever. Their milk ran freely, with plenty for cats and children and baby. And though Ned kept watch for many a night, 'Themselves' were seen no more.

Years later, someone took the silver cup to London. From that time on, Ned stayed indoors after dark. When night came he locked the door and took down his accordion. People wondered where he'd learned such strange wild tunes. But only the cows knew that – and they never told anyone.

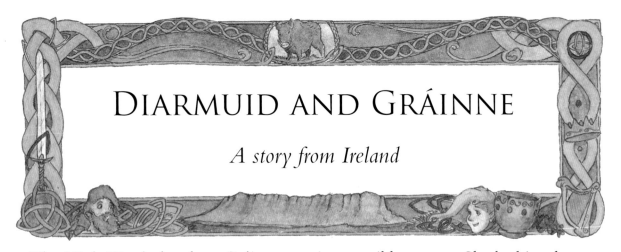

DIARMUID AND GRÁINNE

A story from Ireland

The High King's daughter Gráinne was in a terrible temper. She had just been given the most dreadful news. Her father, Cormac Mac Art, had arranged her marriage – and without her consent! She couldn't understand it. So many men had wanted to marry her – chieftains, warriors, princes. She had refused each one. After all, she was beautiful, clever and talented. The man for her must be someone very special. And now she'd been told she must marry Fionn Mac Cumhail! She flounced down to the lake, away from everyone.

'He must be a thousand years old,' thought Gráinne, as she climbed on the rocks, 'and he's always fighting. My father wants him on his side, and I'm to be the sacrifice! Well I won't have it. I'll only marry the man I choose myself.' She hurled a stone into the lake, splintering the water into a million ripples.

Suddenly she remembered a morning last summer. From her sunroom in Tara she had watched a hurling match. One man surpassed the rest as he hurled the sliothar, fast as an arrow, reckless and bold. She'd wondered – who was the handsome stranger, with his rosy cheeks and curling hair?

'That's the man I'm going to marry,' she'd decided there and then.

Her wedding to Fionn was all arranged however, and in those days fathers had to be obeyed.

A few nights later the wedding feast began. People came to Tara from all the kingdoms. There was boar and venison, wine and mead. Poets and bards recited family histories: their deeds in battle, their bravery and skill. Gráinne didn't listen to a word. Though dressed in jewels and linens, her face was grim. Fionn Mac Cumhail was even worse than she'd feared. Bowed and wrinkled, he was older than her father. Even his son Oisín was older than herself.

Desperately her eyes roved round the room. Was there nobody to save her? Could no one in this company help her to escape? A wolfhound lay dozing by the fire. The men standing nearby laughed and talked. One of them glanced in her direction – and Gráinne's knees went weak. It was the hurler she'd seen last summer, the man who must save her, the only man she'd marry.

She turned to the Druid sitting by her at the table.

'Who are those men over there?' she asked.

'They are the Fianna, Fionn's warriors,' said the Druid, 'and that's Bran, their wolfhound.' He named the warriors one by one – Oisín and Oscar and all the others. But the only one who mattered was the hurler, Diarmuid O'Duibhne.

There was no time to waste. Soon the wedding would take place, and then it would be too late. What should she do? She wished she had the courage to poison Fionn Mac Cumhail. But maybe there was another way …

She called her handmaid over.

'Fetch the jewelled drinking horn from my room,' she whispered, 'and fill it with wine. Then add this sleeping potion – make it good and strong.'

The handmaid obeyed; it wasn't her place to question her mistress.

'Give the cup first to Fionn – say Gráinne sent it. He will pass it round to the others. But the Fianna must not drink it, so take care.'

As the company drank, one by one they fell asleep. Guests nodded at the table, others slumped around the floor. Seeing what was happening, the Fianna grew uneasy. Some reached for their weapons. They paused as Gráinne crossed the hall and stood in front of Diarmuid.

'Diarmuid O'Duibhne,' she said, 'I command you to help me. I will not marry Fionn Mac Cumhail. You are the man I love. Take me away from this place at once.'

The Fianna stepped back, startled. Diarmuid looked in Gráinne's eyes. His heart leaped but he shook his head.

'I cannot help you,' he said. 'You are engaged to Fionn Mac Cumhail. He is my master and I serve him faithfully.'

'My father arranged this marriage without my consent. Fionn is old; I will not marry him. You must help me to escape.'

'I will not do it,' Diarmuid said. 'I would give my life's blood rather than betray my master.'

'Very well,' Gráinne declared. 'Diarmuid O'Duibhne, I put you under *geasa*. Rescue me and take me from this place.'

The men gasped. Diarmuid jumped back as if struck. To be put under *geasa* was very serious. It was a matter of honour, a request that could not be refused.

Diarmuid turned to the others.

'What am I to do?' he asked. 'Fionn is my leader, my hero, my master. How can I betray him? I cannot do as Gráinne asks.'

'She has put you under *geasa*,' said Oisín. 'You know you have no choice.'

'If I bring her away, Fionn will follow and kill us!'

'Go, Diarmuid,' urged Oscar, his dearest friend. 'Take Gráinne with you. We are your friends and will always protect you.'

Diarmuid paused, then turned to Gráinne.

'I will do it,' he said. 'Come, Gráinne.' And taking her hand they slipped out into the dark.

The High King's horses were grazing by the fort. Diarmuid hitched them to the chariot and they started off. They travelled for hours, clattering through the countryside. People stirred in their sleep, wondering who hurried through the night.

Above them the moon gleamed cold as marble. Just as it faded they came to a river.

'Fionn will easily follow the chariot tracks,' Diarmuid said. 'From now on we'll continue on foot.' Taking Gráinne in his arms, he carried her over. They walked for miles till they reached a forest. Diarmuid made a hut from boughs and branches, with a bed of rushes gathered by the lake. While Gráinne rested, he went hunting for food. As soon as they'd eaten, they lay down exhausted. All was silent except for the birds.

★ ★ ★

Back in Tara next morning, word soon got around – Diarmuid and Gráinne were missing. Fionn was furious when the potion wore off; he realised he had been tricked. Burning with jealousy as he thought of his bride, he ordered his trackers to hunt down the pair.

'If you fail to find them, you will pay with your lives!' he screamed.

It wasn't long till they found the trail. They hurried back with the news.

'Diarmuid and Gráinne are in the forest, miles beyond the river.'

'After them at once!' Fionn roared. 'This treachery will end in bloodshed!'

Oisín and the Fianna listened in dismay.

'We must warn Diarmuid,' Oisín whispered. 'We'll send Bran to find him. Then he will know that Fionn is on his way.' Quietly they called the wolfhound and told him what to do. The dog listened, ears erect, then set off at once. In all the world there was none he loved more than Diarmuid O'Duibhne.

In a few hours the wolfhound reached the hut. As soon as Bran woke him, Diarmuid knew they were in danger. Gently he shook Gráinne awake.

'Bran has come to warn us. Fionn is on his way.'

Gráinne gasped in fear. Snatching up their belongings they hurried through the forest.

Time and again the lovers were in danger. Fionn followed them relentlessly. His pirates tried to capture them; he sent vicious dogs to kill them. Diarmuid's godfather Aengus helped when he could; he gave Diarmuid a powerful spear. They came to no harm though, since everywhere they went their friends protected them. They continued on their wanderings, always on guard, always in hiding. In woods and mountains they rambled in secret, through mist and shower, in thunder and snow. They never entered a cave with one opening, nor landed on an island with only one way in. They never ate where they cooked, nor slept where they ate. And every night they stayed in a different place. They tramped all over Ireland, making their bed wherever they could. People whispered to each other when they passed by in darkness, but no one betrayed the desperate young lovers.

Gráinne grew brown and thin with their wanderings, but she never complained. All she needed was the love of Diarmuid, and that she had in full.

★ ★ ★

Years passed, and Gráinne was growing tired. One night she spoke to Diarmuid as they curled up in a cave.

'This is no way to live, like hunted animals. We are both of royal families; we have gold, we have friends. Let us ask Fionn and my father to forgive us. Then we can settle down in a home of our own.'

Diarmuid too was tired of running, of always being on guard.

'You're right,' he said at last. 'I'll go to Aengus. He will speak to your father and to Fionn Mac Cumhail.'

Aengus agreed to their plan. He went first to Gráinne's father, Cormac Mac Art. Gladly Cormac forgave the pair, for he loved his daughter. Next Aengus spoke to Fionn Mac Cumhail.

'It is time for this foolishness to end,' he said. 'In the old days, Diarmuid O'Duibhne helped you in battle. He protected you from enemies; he hunted by your side. You can get another wife. Let Diarmuid and Gráinne live in peace for the rest of their lives.'

Fionn thought it over. He was old and tired of chasing, and much time had passed.

'Very well,' he agreed at last.

Diarmuid and Gráinne were delighted when Aengus brought the news. At last they could relax. They went to live in the lands of the O'Duibhne. There they built a fort, which they called Rath Gráinne. They had four sons and eventually a daughter. The love between them never faded but grew stronger by the day. They had gold and silver, cattle and sheep. Diarmuid still went hunting in the mountains and woods. Only one thing troubled Gráinne.

Long ago, Diarmuid had been given a warning. An evil spell was cast on him while he was very young. This spell declared that, some day, a boar would kill him. Whenever he went hunting, Gráinne lived in fear.

One day she watched as her children played. She thought of her father. She'd never seen him since the night they'd left Tara. She spoke to Diarmuid as they sat by the fire.

'It bothers me that my father has never been to our home. He's the High King of Ireland and our children's grandfather. We should welcome him here.'

'Though he was once against me, I will welcome him for your sake,' Diarmuid answered.

'As for Fionn Mac Cumhail,' Gráinne continued, 'he has surely forgiven us and should be invited too. We will have a feast to win back his friendship.'

'Because he was my enemy, I've kept well away from him,' Diarmuid replied, 'but if it pleases you, we'll invite him to our home.'

Gráinne was delighted and planned a great feast, so enormous it took a whole year to prepare. Messengers were sent to Tara to invite the High King. Fionn too was asked to come. They arrived one afternoon – the High King with his kinsmen, Fionn and the Fianna. They spent a year at Rath Gráinne, feasting and hunting. Gráinne was overjoyed to see her father again, while he was delighted with his five grandchildren. Fionn was very old now and seemed happy to make peace.

Late one night, a hunting horn blasted through the darkness. Diarmuid jumped up from his sleep.

'Someone's hunting on Ben Bulben!' he declared. 'I must go and join them.'

'It's the middle of the night, Diarmuid,' Gráinne said, 'go back to sleep.'

A few hours later the horns rang out again.

'Who could be hunting so late?' Diarmuid wondered. 'I must go and see.'

'Diarmuid, it's still dark and the night is misty. Come back to bed.'

Once more, Diarmuid went to sleep. But when the horns blared at daybreak, he could no longer wait.

'Bring your best weapons,' said Gráinne, as Diarmuid got ready.

'I'll only take the light ones,' Diarmuid said, 'I'm just going out to see what's happening.'

'Oh Diarmuid! Bring Aengus's spear, I fear there will be trouble!'

'Don't worry. What danger could there be in a little morning hunt?'

He kissed her gently and went out into the dawn.

Following the horns' blast, Diarmuid clambered up Ben Bulben. There he found Fionn Mac Cumhail, alone with Bran.

'The Fianna have been hunting all night,' Fionn told him. 'The hounds have found the scent of the Wild Boar of Ben Bulben. He's a savage beast who slaughters on sight. Look! There he is! Let us leave here at once.'

'I will not go,' Diarmuid said, 'but leave Bran to protect me.' He did not want to be a coward before Fionn.

'I will not,' Fionn replied. 'The boar attacked him earlier; he's lucky to be alive.'

And he hurried away, dragging Bran after him.

Diarmuid was dismayed as the boar came closer – it was gigantic! Only then did he remember Gráinne's advice. His best weapons were at home, and those he had with him were almost useless. The boar came roaring towards him, eyes glittering with rage. As the beast charged, Diarmuid flung his spear. It bounced harmlessly off its forehead. The boar turned and charged again, mouth frothing, bristles stiff. Diarmuid slashed with his sword, but it broke in two. Savagely the boar rushed and flung him to the ground, gashing him open with its vicious tusks. As his blood poured out around him, Diarmuid snatched the broken sword. With an almighty effort he pierced the boar's neck. Shrieking in agony, the boar fell dead beside him.

Within minutes the Fianna arrived. They were horrified to find Diarmuid lying gored and bleeding. But Fionn Mac Cumhail smiled.

'You're not so handsome now, my friend. What woman would look at you, now your beauty's gone?'

'You have the power to heal me, Fionn,' Diarmuid gasped.

'How should I heal you?' asked Fionn.

'Have you forgotten your gift? Anyone who drinks water from your hands will be healed.'

Fionn shrugged but went to a nearby well. Cupping his hands with water he started back with the drink. But it slipped through his fingers.

'You let the water spill,' Diarmuid whispered.

'Why should I heal you? You stole Gráinne from me,' Fionn declared.

'She put me under *geasa* – I had no choice. Now bring me the water or I will surely die.'

Again Fionn went to fetch the drink, and again the water trickled from his hands. The Fianna were furious when they saw his tricks.

'You forget how Diarmuid once fought by your side,' they told him. 'He defended and protected you, your best and bravest warrior.'

Fionn's grandson Oscar strode up and stood in front of him.

'If you don't try to save him I will kill you myself!' he swore.

When Fionn heard this he was afraid, since Oscar was young and strong. He rushed away at once. But when he returned, Diarmuid O'Duibhne was dead …

Oscar glared at Fionn.

'I wish I was dead instead of Diarmuid,' he said, 'the noblest of all the Fianna, our friend, our defender. You could have saved him if you helped him in time. And now it's too late.'

Then the Fianna let out three great shouts that sounded to the heavens. Laying their cloaks over Diarmuid's body, they left him there on the hill. With bitter tears they followed Fionn as he headed back to Gráinne. She saw them coming from a long way off. When they told her Diarmuid was dead, sorrow overpowered her. She rocked back and forth tearing at her hair. So piercing were her cries that they echoed to the mountains. People came running to hear the dreadful news. They mourned for Diarmuid who had died on Ben Bulben. Some said he died by jealousy, but others said he died for love.

★ ★ ★

All this occured a long, long time ago. What happened next no one knows for certain. But Diarmuid and Gráinne will never be forgotten. The places where they rested are known to this day, their tragic story still remembered after seventeen hundred years.

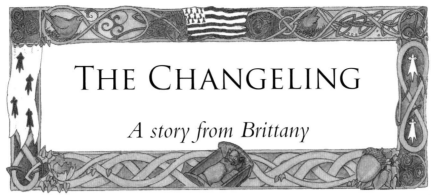

THE CHANGELING

A story from Brittany

Light spilled in the window as Elen opened the shutters. It was Monday and there was washing to be done. That meant washtubs and soapsuds and trips to the fountain. But first there was Loic to look after, Loic – the happiest, most beautiful, most wonderful baby in the world. Elen tiptoed to the cradle for a peep. She loved to watch him sleeping – mouth pink as flowers, cheeks rosy and round. Morvan laughed when she said such silly things.

'Of course he's a handsome fellow! Just look at his father!'

But now Morvan was gone ploughing with the neighbours. There was no one to tease her as she looked in at her son.

'Up you get, little one, time for breakfast. Come to Mama.' She lifted up the warm bundle and cuddled him. He grabbed her curls with small, fat fingers.

'No, no, naughty boy! You must not pull Mama's hair.' Settling back in the chair, she began to feed him. It would be such fun when he learned to talk, but he was too small yet.

Elen loved this time each morning. As Loic fed, she looked around her. Sunlight gleamed on the cradle, carved all over with flowers and patterns. Morvan had made it in the waiting months. On the hearth, Henri the cat sat washing his face.

'How peaceful it all is, and how lucky I am,' thought Elen. 'I have a husband who loves me, a beautiful baby and our own little house.' She did not notice the dark shadow lingering by the window …

As soon as Loic was fed and washed, she put him back in the cradle.

'Now, little man,' she said, 'Mama has to go to the fountain for water. I will only be a minute. Be a good boy and don't cry. When I come back we will

make pretty bubbles.' Then, picking up her buckets, she hurried off.

It was spring and all the birds in Brittany were singing. The cherry trees were in bloom. Seagulls swooped and wheeled on the horizon, following the ploughs. She could see Morvan in the distance with the horses. He would not be home till evening.

'I'll make pork stew for dinner,' she thought as she filled the buckets. 'And if there's time, I'll make crêpes. Morvan loves them with honey. But first there's the washing.' Making her plans, she turned back for the house.

She had scarcely taken a step when a bird flew down at her feet.

'Elen, Elen! Hurry, hurry, hurry!

There's trouble waiting, worry, worry, worry.'

Elen paused for a moment, then shook her head.

'How silly of me!' she said to herself. 'I thought that bird was speaking, that he called my name.' She carried on along the path, grass brushing her skirt as she walked. But the bird flew ahead of her and landed in a bush.

'Elen, Elen! Hurry, hurry, hurry!

There's trouble waiting, worry, worry, worry.'

Elen stopped again.

'Nonsense!' she thought. 'Birds can't speak, I must be imagining things.' But all the same she quickened her step. Once more the bird flew ahead of her, landing now on a cherry bough.

'Elen, Elen! Hurry, hurry, hurry!

There's trouble waiting, worry, worry, worry.'

Now greatly alarmed, Elen started to run. Water slopped from the buckets as she dashed for the house. Not yet at the door, she heard a terrible screeching. She flung the door open and blundered in. After the sunlight all was dark within, but she knew at once that something was terribly wrong. The fire was out, the cat was spitting, while from the cradle came fearful screams. What on earth was the matter? Had something stung Loic? Had the cat frightened him?

She ran to pick him up. But when she looked in the cradle she almost fainted.

Instead of rosy Loic, there lay a horrible baby. Black eyes glared from a twisted face, its skin withered and grey and wrinkled. Claws gripped the covers, tearing them to shreds. Scream after scream ripped through the kitchen.

'Oh mercy! Oh mercy, what has happened, what's happened? Oh Loic! Loic! What happened while I was gone? My beautiful baby! What has changed you so?' She went to pick the creature up, thinking she could soothe it, but something held her back. She could not bear to touch the scrawny thing.

Outside the wind howled round the house, shutters banged, cold crept round the room. Elen dropped to her knees while the screaming went on and on.

'Oh hush, hush. Stop screaming, please stop,' she cried. 'What shall I do? Oh what shall I do? If only it would stop screaming! I can't think clearly.' She covered her ears with her hands.

'Morvan! I'll call Morvan! Morvan will help me. He will know what to do. But how shall I fetch him? He's away in the fields and I dare not leave.' Wildly she glanced around. Her eyes fell on the hunting-horn hung over the mantelpiece. Climbing on a chair, she snatched it down and darted outside. Screams followed her as she blew with all her might:

'Parp pa parp pa parp parp parp!

Morvan, Morvan, come home, come home!

Parp pa parp pa parp parp parp!

I need you, Morvan, come home, come home!'

As the horn echoed across the fields, one of the ploughmen had paused for a drink.

'What's this I hear?' he wondered. 'It sounds like a hunting-horn but it's not the hunting season.' He called to the others to listen.

'It's Elen!' cried Morvan. 'That's my father's hunting-horn – I'd know it anywhere. Something's wrong! I must go home.' And dropping the horses' reins he rushed away. Before he reached the fountain he could hear the screaming.

Elen came running towards him, eyes wild with terror.

'Morvan, Morvan, something terrible has happened!' she sobbed. She gasped out her story as they ran for the house. Morvan got there first. When he looked in the cradle he almost collapsed. But he guessed at once what had happened.

'Be quiet!' he shouted to the creature. 'Stop that racket at once. There'll be no food or drink for you if you don't stop this minute!' Immediately, the screaming stopped.

'Oh, Morvan!' cried Elen. 'How can you shout at Loic so?'

Morvan drew her away from the cradle.

'That's not Loic,' he whispered. 'Don't you see – the fairies have stolen him and left another in his place. That creature is a changeling!'

At this, Elen's knees went weak; she sank into the chair. Fairies loved human babies. They sometimes stole them, replacing them with their own nasty creatures. Such babies were known as changelings.

'Stolen Loic? Oh my poor baby! But how can we know for sure?' She rocked back and forth in the chair. 'What shall we do? Oh Loic, Loic, my darling little boy! What shall we do, Morvan, what shall we do?'

'Shhh!!' whispered Morvan. 'You must pretend that you don't know what's happened. We'll feed and care for this – this creature till we think of a plan.'

'I can't take care of it!' gasped Elen, horrified. 'How can I feed or wash such a hideous thing? I want my baby back, my own baby Loic!'

'Hush, love, don't worry. We'll work something out. I'll stay at home today.'

They spent the day looking after the creature. The changeling screamed for hours, hardly ever sleeping. Howling and snarling, it snatched food from their hands. No sooner had it finished eating than it screamed again. There was no washing done, no dinner prepared. All they had for supper was cold meat and bread.

When night came, they got no sleep. They shut the door on the old box bed, but still they heard the screams. There was nowhere else to put the cradle, since the house had just one room. At dawn, Morvan stirred up the fire. He warmed some milk and fed the creature. Only then did it stop screeching.

'What am I to do?' he thought. 'I can't leave Elen alone with the creature, but I need to get back to work.' She lay exhausted, sleeping at last for a few precious minutes.

Just then, someone tapped quietly at the door. The ploughmen stood outside, looking shy and awkward.

'Is something wrong?' their leader asked. 'We'll help you if we can.'

Morvan closed the door behind him. In a low voice, he explained what had happened. Even as he spoke, the screaming started again.

Old Nikolaz came forward.

'I have knowledge of such matters,' he said. 'Let me see for myself.' He stepped inside and looked in the cradle, then shook his head.

'A right nasty one you have there,' he said, when they were outside again. 'But I know just what to do. Send your wife out to me and I'll explain what must be done.'

Elen stumbled outside, white-faced and frightened.

'There's no doubt about it, that creature is a changeling,' Nikolaz said. 'There's only one way to solve this.' He paused for a moment.

'Has Loic started talking yet?' he asked.

'N–no, he's too young: he can only babble.'

'I thought so. But that ugly thing in there is well able to talk. You must trick it into speaking.' He leaned closer to whisper. 'If you make that brat say something that no baby could know, it will prove it's a changeling. The fairies will realise they can't fool you anymore.'

'But how can I do that?' sobbed Elen, wringing her hands in despair. 'It hardly ever stops screaming – my ears ache just from listening.'

'When evening comes, prop it up in the cradle,' Nikolaz said. 'Get an egg-shell and fill it with meat. The changeling will ask you what you are doing. Tell it you are cooking a meal for ten ploughmen.'

'A meal for ten ploughmen? I'll do as you say. But what then?'

'You'll understand by what it says that this is no baby.' He paused for a moment. 'Take it outside that instant, and leave it for the fairies. They'll soon know they can't trick Elen and Morvan. When they hear it screaming, your child will be returned.'

'I'll do as you say,' Elen said, 'but I'm so scared.'

Nikolaz took her hands in his.

'Have courage. Don't pretend you notice anything, just do your usual chores. We'll work close by today so Morvan will be near you. Soon your child will be home again.'

All that day, Elen tried to do as Nikolaz had said. She washed clothes, swept the floor, polished the linen-chest. The changeling screamed most of the day, but sometimes it stopped to watch her. When evening came, she propped it up with pillows, moving the cradle close to the table. With trembling hands she broke an egg into a bowl. Then taking the eggshell, she filled it with pork.

'What are you doing, mother? What are you doing?' the changeling demanded. Elen shuddered at the deep harsh voice. This was no baby just learning to talk.

'What am I doing? I'm making dinner for ten ploughmen,' she answered.

'A meal for ten ploughmen … in an eggshell … How can you do that?'

'Don't you see me doing it?' Elen answered. 'When I fill the eggshell I will cook it on the coals. It will feed the ten ploughmen when they come in.'

The changeling grinned.

'Well, well,' it said,

'I've seen the acorn before the oak

and the egg before the hen,

but I've never seen an eggshell

that will feed ten men!'

And it laughed so hard that the cradle rocked on the floor.

Elen dropped the eggshell on the table.

'I've got you now, you nasty creature!' she yelled. 'If you're old enough to have seen an acorn grow into an oak, then you're no baby! You're hundreds of years old! I know just who you are, you wicked changeling! Morvan, Morvan!' she shouted as she ran from the house. The creature shrieked as he came running, but Morvan paid no attention. He snatched up the cradle and raced down the path. He left it under the cherry trees where all the petals tumbled.

'Call for your own kind,' he ordered, 'and get back to where you came from! And never enter this house again!'

Dashing back to the cottage, he locked the door and bolted it, then closed the shutters tight. Elen built a huge fire, sparks sweeping up the chimney. Henri hissed and humped his back.

Morvan held Elen close. For hours they listened to the bloodcurdling screams.

'Oh, please make something come for it,' sobbed Elen. 'Please make it go away and give me back my boy.'

They clung to one another all that long night, as the screaming went on and on and on. At last, worn out, they fell asleep.

Just as dawn crept through the shutters, Morvan woke. The crying had stopped. Gently he shook Elen awake. They listened while a cock crowed, a pigeon cooed, a dog barked in the distance. They looked at one another. Quietly they unbolted the door. Clutching hands, they tiptoed down the path. The cradle stood where they'd left it. Fearfully they peeped in. A round, rosy face was smiling up at them.

'Loic! Oh Loic! My baby! My baby!' Elen snatched him up, hugging and kissing him and crying by turns. Loic laughed as he reached for her curls.

All had happened just as Nikolaz said, and soon everything was the same as before. The old box bed stood with door wide open. Sunlight gleamed on the cradle, carved all over with flowers and patterns. Henri slept peacefully on the hearth. And as for Loic – he grew into a strong, handsome boy. Elen never left him alone in the house again, no, not even for a minute. Not until he was old enough to go ploughing with his father, when seagulls swooped on the horizon and the cherry-trees bloomed.

CLEVER MORAG

A story from Scotland

The King of the Fairies was grumpy. His tummy rumbled, his legs were weak. Before him on the table were cakes and bread; they lay grey, flat and tasteless on the royal plates.

'I cannot eat this stuff!' he cried. 'How can a king survive on such froth? Tricks and fiddlesticks – get me some real bread!' And he thumped the table till every plate rattled.

'B-b-but your Majesty,' stuttered the butler, 'that's all fairy bakers bake. We only know the ways of nature – the nuts and berries, the sweetness of honeysuckle. We've never mastered the skill of real bread.'

'Then get me someone who has!' roared the king. 'If I don't get some decent bread soon I'll … I'll … I'll throw a tantrum.' And his face went dangerously red.

'Yes, your Majesty, of course, your Majesty,' the butler muttered. He hurried to the kitchen as a plate flew past his head.

'It's no use,' said the butler to the housekeeper. 'The king is in a rage. We can't put it off any longer. We'll have to steal some human's bread.'

'We'll have to *what*?' gasped the housekeeper.

'You heard me. If we don't do something soon, he'll turn us into frogs. I'm certain sure of it.'

They talked and argued till they had a plan. Then calling in the Fairy Troop, they explained what must be done.

'A baker lives on the road to Aberdeen – you'll know his shop by the sign outside. Bring a sack each. Take a loaf from the baker and divide it between you. Bring it here at once. You must be back by breakfast-time.'

The fairies collected bags and sacks. A swirl of wind soon whisked them to the village. There on the square stood the baker's shop. Rows of loaves lined the shelves, ready for the morning. As the baker snored, they loaded up their sacks. Soon they were back in the shadow of the mountains. They crept into bed as the sun came up.

The butler prepared breakfast himself. He toasted the bread, spreading it with honey. The king sniffed as the butler came in.

'Smells good,' he said, tasting a slice.

The butler watched anxiously as the king's face changed.

'Stodge and stuffing!' he roared. 'Is this what humans eat? It's even worse than our own!' And he swept the breakfast to the floor.

'That didn't work,' sighed the butler to the housekeeper. 'We'll have to try someone else.'

'How about old Elspeth who lives beyond the bridge? She's been baking all her life.'

'The very one!' cried the butler. He ran to call the Fairy Troop from their beds.

'We've only gone to sleep,' they grumbled. 'Now you want us to go out again, and in broad daylight.'

'It's for the king,' he explained, 'and if you get enough bread, you can keep some for yourselves.'

Muttering and mumbling, they set off again. Crossing the bridge to Elspeth's house, they hid behind some foxgloves. Soon Elspeth came out with freshly-baked bread. She left it cooling on a rack, then tottered back inside. Silently the Fairy Troop left their hiding-place. Stuffing their sacks, they hurried home.

Next day at breakfast, the butler sliced the bread. Some he cut in wedges, some he spread with jam. The king licked his lips when the butler came in.

'Looks good,' he said as he ate a bit. The butler watched anxiously as the king's face changed.

'Slime and slither!' he bellowed. 'Who baked this stuff? It's even worse than the baker's!' And with a roar, he pushed the table over.

'Now what?' groaned the butler, when the mess was cleaned up.

'There's only one thing for it,' said the housekeeper. 'We'll try red-haired Morag. She lives across the valley with her husband, the piper. I've often heard it said that she makes fantastic bread.'

The Fairy Troop was ordered to Morag's house. They waited and waited, but no bread appeared outside.

One brave fairy stole indoors in the shadows. The poor, bare kitchen was spotless and neat. The floor was swept, a small baby gurgled in the cradle. Morag herself was busy at the table. Up since dawn, her bread was long since ready. As she sliced and buttered, crumbs tumbled to the floor. The brave fairy snatched them up and tossed them in her sack.

'That's funny,' said Morag to herself. 'I thought I saw a shadow by the door.' She went to look, but there was nothing to be seen – just a puff of summer dust on the road.

Next morning, the butler laid the crumbs on a plate. He didn't toast them or slice them or sweeten them. The king frowned when the butler came in.

'What's this?' he asked. 'Only crumbs for a king?' But he put them in his mouth.

The butler watched anxiously as the king's face changed.

'By all that's wonderful!' he shouted, 'This bread is fantastic! I want more, more, more! Where did you find such gorgeous, luscious crumbs?'

So the butler explained.

'Bring this Morag here at once! Kidnap her if you must. This woman will be our Royal Baker! Fetch her instantly if you value your life!'

Now it's one thing to steal a few crumbs from people. It's another thing altogether to steal a human being.

'We'll have to cast a spell,' said the butler, 'and it had better be good. I've heard it said that this Morag is a very clever person.'

Mumbling, the housekeeper rummaged in her cupboard. A pinch of this, a scrap of that, a chant of ancient magic …

Back in her cottage, Morag suddenly felt drowsy. She sat down by the hearth.

'It must be the weather,' she thought. 'I'll just have a little nap while the baby is asleep.'

★ ★ ★

Morag was astonished when she woke. How had she come to be in this strange place? Was she dreaming? No, the small chairs and table were made of solid wood. Tiny copper pans twinkled on their hooks. And the little man who spoke to her was sure of his words.

'Morag,' he said, 'you are in the Fairy King's kitchen. You've been chosen by His Majesty to be the Royal Baker. It's a wonderful honour to be selected by the king. You will remain here forever. Now get to work at once, please. The king has demanded your bread for his supper.'

Morag gasped. Her cheeks flared pink with temper, her hair flamed red with rage.

'What cheek! Who does he think he is?' she muttered to herself. She thought of her baby – the darling! – alone in his cradle. She thought of Duncan her husband, at the Fair in Aberdeen. What would he think when he came home and found his wife gone? How could she escape? She would have to think carefully, for fairies were tricky.

'There'll be no baking done till you bring me my baby,' she declared. 'The poor, darling creature is at home all by himself.'

'Very well,' said the butler, and he called the Fairy Troop. As they started off, Morag thought and thought. Her foot tapped, her fingers drummed the table.

'You mustn't do that,' said the butler, 'the king can't stand noise. Fairies' ears are very sensitive.'

When the baby arrived, he was roaring for a feed. Morag took her time as she fed and cuddled him. At last he went to sleep.

'Now get to work,' said the butler, as soon as she was finished.

'There'll be no baking done till I have my spoon and mixing-bowl,' Morag said. 'I cannot make bread without my own bits and pieces.' So the Fairy Troop was ordered off for mixing-bowl and spoon.

'There'll be no baking done till I have my jug and rolling-pin,' she said, when they returned. 'I cannot make bread without my own utensils.'

'Very well,' sighed the butler. 'But then you must begin.'

Back came the fairies with jug and rolling pin. But Morag wasn't ready yet.

'How can I make bread,' she asked, 'without eggs or flour or milk? Your fairies must go to my cottage and collect them.'

Grumbling and grousing, the Fairy Troop departed. As they set off for the valley, Morag plotted and planned. She hummed and muttered, she whistled through her teeth. The butler hushed her as he listened at the door. But all was still; the king was having his afternoon nap.

How the fairies complained as they hauled the crock of milk! As for rolling eggs uphill … They arrived back sticky and splattered with egg-yolk.

'Now begin,' ordered the butler. 'The king has only had crumbs for breakfast – he'll be absolutely starving.'

There was no excuse left so Morag set to work. She poured and mixed and stirred and battered, clattering dishes, pounding and kneading. Nervously the butler twisted his fingers

'Can't you stop that racket?' he asked. 'If the king is disturbed, he'll turn us into frogs!'

Morag thought quickly.

'I'm sorry,' she said, 'but I'm rather upset. I can't help thinking about all my animals. There's nobody to feed them or keep them from straying. You must bring them here.' And, folding her arms, she sat down on the largest chair.

'I can't do that!' gasped the butler. 'Where would we put them?'

'That's your problem,' Morag said. She lay back on the cushions and began to sing. 'Follow my Highland Laddie' echoed through the kitchen.

'Hush! Be quiet!' begged the butler. 'I'll do my best, but please, please don't make that noise.'

'Noise indeed!' Morag snapped, tossing her head. But she stopped singing and pretended to doze.

Once more the Fairy Troop was ordered to work. Such a dreadful time they had! At last they returned – with seven sheep, six lambs, five hens, four kittens, three cats, two dogs and one fuzzy duckling. They all squashed together into the palace kitchen. With the baaing and clucking and hissing and barking, of course the baby woke. He began to scream for all his worth.

'Stop it, oh stop the racket!' the butler pleaded. 'If the king hears, he'll turn us into toads!'

'I need my husband's help,' Morag said. 'He'll be coming home now from the Fair of Aberdeen. You must meet him on the road.'

The butler clicked his fingers for the Fairy Troop.

'No!' they screeched together. 'We're exhausted, we can't lift a wing.'

'In that case, there'll be no bread baked,' Morag said. 'I'll not do another thing till Duncan steps into this kitchen.'

'Alright, alright! I'll fetch him here myself!' snapped the butler. Frantic with worry he hurried off. Morag stoked the fire to heat the oven. She washed the utensils and wiped down the table. Next it was time to feed the baby. She had just finished when Duncan walked in. Leaving down his bagpipes he stared in astonishment.

'What's happening? What's going on?' asked the poor, bewildered fellow.

'I'll explain later,' Morag hissed in his ear. 'Now strike up a tune while I finish this bread. And play as loudly as you can!'

Immediately Duncan started up his pipes. First there was a droning, next a little squawking. Then 'Scotland the Brave' streamed across the kitchen. The baby shouted and clapped his hands, the Fairy Troop screeched. Skirls of bagpipes rang out across the palace. The housekeeper screamed and ran from the kitchen, flattening the butler who was just rushing in. Duncan started on 'Scots Wha Hae' as Morag put the bread in the oven.

The door crashed open, the king charged in. His crown hung over one eye, his fists were in his ears.

'Out!' he bellowed, 'out, out, out! Get out at once, before I turn you into snakes! Clear off the lot of you! I never want to see you again!' He snatched up bowl and rolling pin and flung them out the door. Jug and spoon came hurtling after.

Morag grabbed the baby while Duncan grabbed the cradle. Picking up their things they started off home – with seven sheep, six lambs, five hens, four kittens, three cats, two dogs and one fuzzy duckling. As they walked along, Morag told her story.

'Clever Morag,' Duncan laughed, 'only you could fool the fairies!'

Next morning, a fairy tiptoed into Morag's kitchen. There was a message from the king. He was very sorry for all that had happened, but Morag's bread was the best he'd ever tasted. If she left some out for him each week, she would be well rewarded. So ever since she leaves her bread on the north windowsill. And every week a gold coin is left in its place.

The little kitchen is no longer poor and bare. Duncan still plays the bagpipes at the Fair of Aberdeen. And as for Morag – her cheeks flare pink with happiness and her hair flames red with love.

ABOUT THE STORIES

Conor the Brave – Ireland

There is a great wealth of old tales in Ireland, some going back for thousands of years. In ancient times, bards and storytellers were highly regarded. Though the stories were passed down by word of mouth, many were eventually written down and translated into English. This story is based on a tale called 'Gilla na Chreck an Gour', from *Legendary Fictions* by Patrick Kennedy, published in 1891. 'The Lad with the Goat Skin' was also retold by Joseph Jacobs in his book *Celtic Fairy Tales*, first published in 1892. A version of the story is well known in other cultures.

Before electricity, soda bread was baked in an iron oven on the open hearth. Boxty is a traditional potato bread. Both breads are still made in Ireland.

The Seal Catcher's Story – Scotland

This story comes from the north of Scotland. It was also well known to other Celtic peoples living on islands and by sea shores. Many of them believed that seals could shed their skins, and so become human. Such creatures were called 'selkies', from the Scots word selch, meaning seal. In 1901, George Douglas published *Scottish Fairy and Folk Tales*. The stories contained in the book were collected from various sources in rural Scotland almost a century before that, and were ancient tales even then. 'The Sealcatcher's Story' is based on a tale from this collection.

Blaanid's Secret – The Isle of Man

In this story, Blaanid has to solve a riddle to get what she needs. The telling of riddles was greatly enjoyed by people in past times. They feature in tales from many different cultures. A similar story is 'Rumpelstiltskin', collected in Germany by the Brothers Grimm, while 'Ridire of Riddles' was well known in the West Highlands of Scotland. Cronk ny Arrey Laa is a hill in the south-west of the Isle of Man. The name is said to mean 'The Hill of Day Watch', a place where sentries watched for Viking invaders.

A settle was a seat that was a bench by day and could be used as a bed at night. A skein is a coil of yarn or thread. In the nineteenth century, Sophia Morrison collected many folk tales from local people in the Isle of Man. This retelling is based on 'The Lazy Wife', from her collection *Manx Fairy Tales*, published in 1911.

The Magic Pail – Cornwall

Long ago, the people of Cornwall were aware of many different kinds of fairies, including piskies, knockers, hobgoblins and others. They referred to them as the 'Small People'. The mine mentioned in the story is thought to be the Ding Dong mine in west Cornwall. The story, however, is based on one from *The Piskey Purse – Legends and Tales of North Cornwall*. These were collected locally by Enys Tregarthen and published in 1906.

A cairn is a pile of stones, marking an ancient burial place. Some people believed that such a place was the entrance to the fairy world. Cairns can be found throughout the Celtic lands and were places to be respected and sometimes feared.

The Red Dragon – Wales

King Gwrtheyrn is thought to have lived in the third century AD in what is now Wales. He was also known as Vortigern and was said to have been very cruel. He invited the Saxons to Britain to help him fight against his enemies. In time the Saxons became very powerful and turned against him.

The story of the Red Dragon, based on Celtic legends, was written down by Nennius, a Christian monk, in 800 AD. It was retold in medieval times by Geoffrey of Monmouth, a Welsh priest. The tale was included in a manuscript called 'The Mabinogion' in 1795 and the collection translated into English in the nineteenth century. This retelling is based on a story from *Welsh Fairy Tales* by William Elliot Griffis, published in 1921.

The Silver Cup – The Isle of Man

In the Isle of Man in times past, people referred to the fairies as 'Themselves' or 'the Small People', believing that this was more respectful. It was important not to annoy the fairies and to avoid their haunts if possible. Such beliefs were handed down from one generation to the next. Similar beliefs were held in other Celtic countries. The search for a trophy is also known in Scotland in the story 'The Page Boy and the Silver Goblet.' 'The Silver Cup' is based on a story of the same name, collected by Sophia Morrison and published in *Manx Fairy Tales* in 1911. '*Shoh slaynt*' is a Welsh phrase meaning 'good health' or 'cheers'.

Diarmuid and Gráinne – Ireland

This story is one of the oldest tales told in Ireland and is widely known in Scotland also. It was first referred to in *The Book of Leinster,* which was written around 1100. The Fianna, of which Diarmuid was a member, were believed to have lived in Ireland in the third century AD and their stories were recounted far and wide. A fuller account of this tragic tale, '*Tóraíocht Dhiarmada agus Ghráinne*', or 'The Pursuit of Diarmuid and Gráinne', survives from the seventeenth century.

Hurling is an ancient game still played and highly popular in Ireland. The ball, or sliothar, is made of leather and hit with a hurley stick. Druids were wise pagan priests, said to have magic powers. To be put under *geasa* was a serious obligation to carry out a request. The places where Diarmuid and Gráinne slept and rested can be seen all over Ireland to this day. They are mentioned in several placenames. Diarmuid and

Gráinne had many other adventures, which are not included in this retelling.

The Changeling – Brittany

'Changelings' are well known in Celtic lands. Many believed that the fairies stole humans, usually boy babies, and replaced them with their own. Of course the fairy babies were always ugly, cranky and difficult. Such infants were known as 'changelings'. 'The Brewery of Eggshells', a similar story, was widely told in Wales and Ireland. Scotland has 'The Smith and the Fairies,' while 'The Fairy Child of Close ny Lheiy' is found in the Isle of Man. 'The Changeling' is based on a tale from *Folk Tales of Brittany* by Elsie Masson, published in 1929. These were collected from old folk songs and legends in the Breton language.

Clever Morag – Scotland

In Celtic folklore, there are constant struggles between humans and the many different beings around them. In Scotland these include brownies, mermaids, selkies, roans, fairies, giants, witches, dragons, kelpies, ogres, monsters, trolls, sea-devils, water-horses, hags... In this story a feisty woman gets the better of the fairies through her cleverness. The tunes mentioned are well-known Scottish airs. The bagpipes have been considered Scotland's national instrument for several hundred years.

The story is based on 'The Woman who Flummoxed the Fairies' from *Heather and Broom- Tales of the Scottish Highland*s. This was a collection of tales compiled by Sorche Nic Leodhas and published by Holt in 1961. Though born in Ohio, U.S.A. in 1898, she heard these tales from Scottish relations at family gatherings. They in turn learned them from their ancestors, who heard them from wandering storytellers in the Scottish Highlands.